My name is Barry Allen, and I'm the fastest man alive. A particle accelerator explosion sent a bolt of lightning into my lab one night, shattering a shelf of containers and dousing me in electricity and chemicals. When I woke up from a coma nine months later, I found I was gifted with superspeed.

Since then, I've worked to keep Central City and its people safe from those with evil intent. With the help of my friends Caitlin and Cisco at S.T.A.R. Labs; my girlfriend, Iris; her brother, Wally; and my adoptive father, Joe, I've battled time travelers, mutated freaks, and metahumans of every stripe.

I've tried to reconcile my past, learned some tough lessons, and—most important of all—never, ever stopped moving forward.

I am . . .

THE FLASH

BY BARRY LYGA

1SH

JOHNNY QUICK

AMULET BOOKS

NEW YORK

Dedicated to Marc Nathan, who gave me the key
to the comic book store. Quite literally.

Cataloging-in-Publication Data has been applied for
and may be obtained from the Library of Congress.

ISBN 978-1-4197-2865-5

Cover illustration by César Moreno
Book design by Chad W. Beckerman

Amulet Books and Amulet Paperbacks are
registered trademarks of Harry N. Abrams, Inc.

Printed and bound in USA
10 9 8 7 6 5 4 3 2 1

Amulet Books are available at special discounts when purchased in quantity for premiums
and promotions as well as fundraising or educational use. Special editions can also be
created to specification. For details, contact specialsales@abramsbooks.com or the
address below.

ABRAMS The Art of Books
195 Broadway, New York, NY 10007
abramsbooks.com

PREVIOUSLY IN

Barry Allen seemed to be on top of the world. His love life is going just great, thanks to his amazing girlfriend, Iris. And his friends and family—tech genius Cisco, medical whiz Caitlin, adoptive father, Joe, fellow speedster Wally, and irascible H.R.—make it easy to be a hero.

But then came Hocus Pocus, the crazed "magician" with tech so advanced no one could figure it out. He made the Flash his puppet and ran roughshod over Central City until Barry and his friends finally figured out a way to stop him and lock him up in the Pipeline.

Only for Hocus Pocus to vanish mere hours later. Which should be impossible.

Worse yet, someone or something in the sewers called "Earthworm" is killing people . . . and Barry's repeated absences from work have put his job at the Central City Police Department on the line.

The only way The Flash can solve all of these problems is by tackling one at a time . . .

PROLOGUE

BENEATH THE CITY, TWO HEARTS beat. One throbbed along at a comfortable pace of seventy-five beats per minute, a rate that would cause neither panic nor even alarm if you were monitoring it.

The other . . . *raced*.

Well over 120 beats per minute. A ferocious, *terrified* heart rate. Unsustainable in the long term.

Herb Shawn, whose heartbeat was the accelerated one, lay terrified in the filth of the tunnels beneath Central City. His eyes had adjusted to what could most charitably be described as murky quarter-light from an old emergency lamp that winked and flickered at random. It wasn't possible to see so much as to perceive vague, moving hazes and glimmering fogs. From the echoes of water and his own panicked breathing, the chamber he was in must have been large, but all he could reckon of it was the wall behind him.

His vision was limited and his hearing brought him only hollow echoes, but his sense of smell was working full-time. More's the pity. The reek of the sewer assailed him; even when he held his breath, it violently insinuated itself into his nostrils like a burrowing groundhog seeking shelter.

He lay half-covered in grimy water, in which floated things he did not want to identify. The cold of the water had settled into his bones; he could barely feel his legs, though he knew they itched to stand, to run.

Not that he could do either. He was shackled to the wall, connected by a hefty chain to a stout U-bolt. He'd tried a few experimental tugs when he'd woken, but the chain had not budged. He was securely held in place. Down here in the dark and the echoey quiet and the stink.

And just then . . . a sound. Something on the farthest periphery of his hearing. But it was there, no doubt. Something moved out there in the water.

A rat? Something else? He'd heard a crazy rumor about some kind of ape or gorilla living in the sewers, but that just had to be nonsense. This whole city had gone crazy ever since that explosion a few years back. People were seeing things every which way they turned. He should have moved by now. Should have moved to Coast City or Star City or even St. Roch. Anywhere was better than—

There. There it was again. Something in the water. Small. A rat. Had to be.

He was both grateful and disgusted at the same time. A rat, even a big one, could be fended off. But what if there were more, lurking just beyond? Could he fight off a swarm of them before—

His heartbeat, already rocketing, leaped even further as a figure swam out of the murk before him, leaning in. In utter terror, he shrieked, screaming loud and long. The sound echoed from the walls, overlapping his own scream, filling his ears to the bursting point.

The figure (the possessor of the other, calmer heartbeat beneath Central City that night) waited patiently until Herb had stopped screaming. It was tall, looming over him, seeming even taller for its thinness and the forced perspective of Herb's position on the ground. It was human but somehow inhuman at the same time. Two arms, two legs, a head, but . . . so tall and so skinny that it seemed more a disjointed skeleton assembled out of parts than a living, breathing organism. Its skin was sallow, the color of old lemons, and its nose was the barest scrap of a bump, the nostrils wide and flaring. Ridges rose from its eyes to the apex of its bald head, furrows of flesh that gave it a demonic appearance.

It wore a shabby coat and threadbare jeans with a long, bedraggled red scarf knotted around its neck. A rat perched on its shoulder, patiently regarding Herb with glittering, hungry eyes.

"Please . . ." Herb whimpered. It was the only word he could conjure in that moment.

The figure leaned in close. Its jaundiced flesh seemed rotten somehow, as though it had died even though the person to whom it clung still lived. As Herb watched, a cluster of worms erupted from the lapel of the figure's jacket and slithered along the fabric.

"Please," he said again.

The man—for it *was* a man, Herb realized, though one more grotesque and misshapen than any he'd ever seen before—tilted his malformed head to one side. The rat chittered softly in his ear.

"You have. Something. I need." The man's voice sounded like a rusty, broken fan, staccato and raspy. "Once I take it from you, you'll be set free. Set free to roam the Upworld again."

The Upworld?

Herb nodded fiercely. He would agree to anything, give up anything, just to get this chain off his wrist and see the sunlight again.

"You can have it. Whatever it is." Herb thought quickly of the contents of his pockets. He had little cash on him, but he would give it all up. His credit cards, too. And his cell phone, of course. It had been soaking in the water for a while now and might not even work, but he would *buy* a new one for this creature if that's what it took.

"Good." The man nodded once, with finality, and produced something from his pocket. "Let's begin."

He leaned in farther—and Herb saw that what he'd withdrawn from his pocket was a surgical scalpel.

Herb screamed again. For a very, very long time.

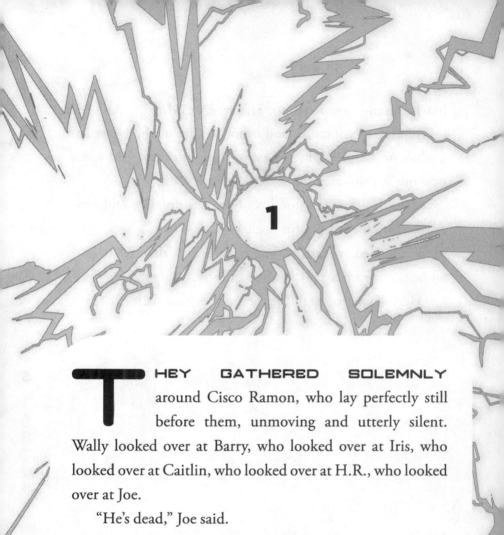

THEY GATHERED SOLEMNLY
around Cisco Ramon, who lay perfectly still
before them, unmoving and utterly silent.
Wally looked over at Barry, who looked over at Iris, who
looked over at Caitlin, who looked over at H.R., who looked
over at Joe.

"He's dead," Joe said.

More silence among those gathered. Then, without
warning, Cisco snorted, a single, loud, nasal blast that
echoed in the medical bay at S.T.A.R. Labs. His body juddered once, then went still and quiet again.

"Dead *tired*," H.R. whispered. He looked around at
the assembled Team Flash. "Well, *I'm* not waking him up."

Cisco had been sleeping for close to twenty-four hours

after a days-long, caffeine-fueled tech binge during which he'd tried to figure out how Hocus Pocus's advanced technology worked. After the magician was captured, Cisco had fallen asleep on one of the beds in the medical bay and he hadn't moved since. Now they needed him awake again. Hocus Pocus had pulled off an impossible disappearing act from the heart of the inescapable Pipeline, and the Flash needed to know *how*.

With a sigh, Barry poked Cisco in the sternum. Cisco grunted, flapped a loose hand in Barry's general direction, then rolled onto his side and kept right on sleeping.

"Poor thing." Caitlin gnawed at her lower lip. "Do we *have* to wake him up?"

"It's been almost a *day*," Wally complained. "I mean, come on. Just open a window and blast some heavy metal."

"We're underground, so the window isn't going to accomplish anything," Iris reminded him. "And Barry's phone is just loaded up with old show tunes, because he's a gigantic nerd like that." She smiled sweetly. "Which I totally love, by the way."

Barry ignored the shot at his musical tastes and considered his friend before him, sleeping the sleep of the just. "There's another way. Let him sleep. It's OK."

"You sure?" Joe asked. "This guy just *vanished*. Last time

Hocus Pocus was at large, he nearly had you bump off an entire baseball stadium full of innocent people."

"He won't catch me with the same tricks twice," Barry said confidently. "Besides," he went on, spinning an object in his hand until it blurred with speed, "I have his 'magic wand.' Wherever he is, Hocus Pocus isn't going to be casting any high-tech 'spells' anytime soon."

As if in agreement, the sleeping Cisco chuckled momentarily, then mumbled, "Well, if you insist, m'lady . . ."

"What *is* he dreaming about?" Wally wondered.

"I don't want to know," Iris said.

In the Cortex, Barry walked Hocus Pocus's wand back and forth along the backs of his fingers. It was an easy bit of sleight of hand that he'd taught himself by practicing thirteen thousand times when he'd had five minutes to kill while Iris got dressed for dinner.

The wand was utterly boring. Unassuming. Slender, it measured perhaps ten inches in length, tapering from a one-inch diameter at its base to a near pencil point at the tip. It gleamed dully in the overhead lighting of the Cortex, its color a flat, metallic gray without seam or break. The whole thing looked as though it had been cast in aluminum, and it weighed next to nothing.

It was the most powerful weapon in the world, as far

as Barry knew. It could project and control nanites that defied the laws of physics and had infected his own brain, making him Hocus Pocus's thrall. And yet there were no buttons or levers or touch pads anywhere on the thing, its technology advanced even beyond what Cisco was capable of.

Iris came up behind him and kneaded his shoulders. "Staring at that thing isn't going to unlock its secrets any faster," she said.

"I just keep thinking . . . It looks so . . . so . . ."

"Innocuous?" she suggested.

He grinned. Trust the journalist to come up with the perfect word. "Yeah. Innocuous. But it caused so much trouble. It almost killed me and so many others. I need to figure out how it works. That might lead the way to Hocus Pocus. So that I can stop him for good." Barry took in a deep breath. "I need to get to Earth 2. Their tech is a little more advanced over there—maybe Harry and Jesse can crack this open and figure it out."

"Once Cisco wakes up, he'll open a breach and get you over there," she told him.

"I don't think I can wait that long." He danced the wand over the back of his hand again. "Who knows where he is, what he's up to, what he's planning. I have to track him down and stop him." Barry snapped his fingers. "And I think I have a way to do it."

Iris blinked. "You have a door to Earth 2 in your pocket somewhere?"

"No. Maybe something better. But let's give Cisco a little while longer and see if he comes to. I want to go see what Madame Xanadu has to say about all of this."

Iris raised her eyebrows. "Really?"

Barry flushed as red as his Flash costume. "Look, it's not that I actually believe she's psychic—"

"Uh-huh."

"—or nonsense like that. I'm a scientist. I don't believe in magic. But she might be a meta and not even realize it. There's *something* to her, and I want to pick her brain about this."

"Can I go with you?"

Now it was Barry's turn to raise his eyebrows. "Really?"

"I've just *got* to see the woman who's made my über-rational boyfriend believe in magic," she cracked, then kissed him quickly before he could splutter a denial.

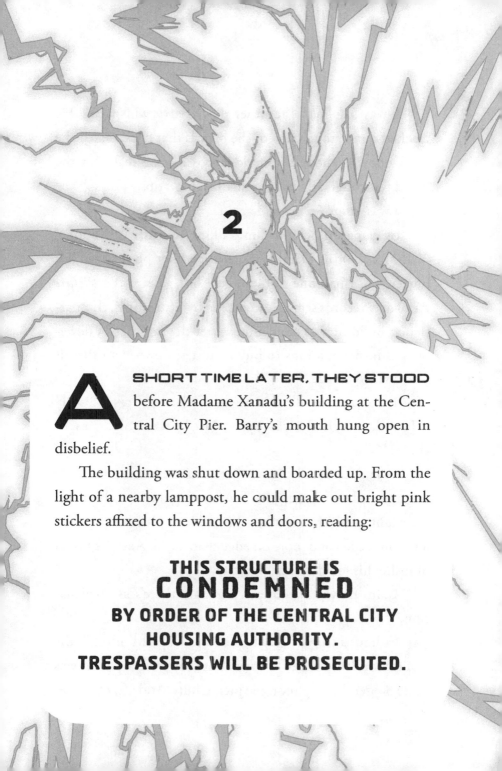

2

A SHORT TIME LATER, THEY STOOD before Madame Xanadu's building at the Central City Pier. Barry's mouth hung open in disbelief.

The building was shut down and boarded up. From the light of a nearby lamppost, he could make out bright pink stickers affixed to the windows and doors, reading:

**THIS STRUCTURE IS
CONDEMNED
BY ORDER OF THE CENTRAL CITY
HOUSING AUTHORITY.
TRESPASSERS WILL BE PROSECUTED.**

"I was just here the other day," Barry whispered. He reached out to touch one of the boards that crisscrossed the front door, as though it couldn't possibly be real. But the wood was rough and solid under his fingertips.

"I was *just here*!" he said again.

Iris came up behind him, talking into her cell phone. "Uh-huh. Got it. Thanks." She slipped her phone into her purse. "So, I had one of the night shift guys at the *Picture News* do a records search. According to city records, this particular building was condemned over the summer. A developer is in negotiations to buy it, tear it down, and turn it into a video arcade."

"I was *just* here!" Barry erupted in protest. "Only a few days ago! It was open! No boards! She was in there!"

Iris laid her hands flat on Barry's chest to calm him. He was agitated and fidgety, his features beginning to blur just the slightest bit. His trials at the hands of Hocus Pocus had left him rattled and more on edge than usual. And the threat of losing his job didn't help, either.

"Calm down, sweetheart. I'm sure there's an explanation."

Without a word, Barry turned and vibrated through the front door. Iris glanced around, but they were alone. It was a late September night on the pier. Chilly. And after the previous evening's assault by Hocus Pocus, not many Central Citizens wanted to hang out at the pier, especially this late at night.

Moments later, he phased through the door again, returning to her side. He was shaken, his eyes wide, his face pallid. "There's nothing in there but dust," he whispered. "A *lot* of dust. Inches thick. More than just a few days' worth. It's like it's been abandoned since—"

"Since last summer?"

He opened his mouth, then closed it. Sighed heavily. "I was in there *so* recently, Iris. I spoke to her."

Iris weighed her words carefully. Barry had been through so much in the past few days, and the next few weren't looking to shape up to be any better. "Maybe you imagined the whole thing," she ventured. "You were under a lot of stress. You had those nanites messing up your brain . . . Maybe Pocus made you *think* you were visiting her—"

"Why would he do that? She gave me advice on how to stop him. She made it *possible* for me to stop him." Barry thumped his palm with his fist. "This doesn't make any sense. Besides, how do you explain this?" He produced a playing card from his pocket and showed it to her. Black and silver threads braided around each other along the outer edge of the card. The remainder of the card was stark white, except for a black speck at the center.

"I chose this card from her deck," Barry said. "And I still have it. I didn't conjure it from thin air. She was *here*."

Iris sighed, relenting. "I can keep digging, see if the property records have any sort of connection to someone with the name *Xanadu* . . ."

"No. No." He kissed her forehead. "Of all the mysteries in my life, this is the one that can wait. No one's life depends on Madame Xanadu's address. C'mon—let's go."

Back at S.T.A.R. Labs, Cisco was still asleep. It had been more than twenty-four hours. The members of Team Flash who were awake gathered in the Cortex. They could barely hear the soft drone of Cisco's snoring from the medical bay.

"This has to be a record," Wally said.

"That's a good point," Joe added. "How long can someone sleep before it starts to become a problem?"

Gnawing on her knuckle, Caitlin sighed. "Sleep *solves* problems for the body. It doesn't cause them. Cisco was fueling himself with caffeine for days to stay awake. Caffeine slams your central nervous system, hard. It blocks the adenosine receptors in your brain so that you don't feel tired. But when it wears off, all that pent-up adenosine floods your brain, and you crash. So he'd feel the crash coming and have more caffeine to stave it off, and the cycle just kept going until finally . . ." She gestured to the sleeping Cisco.

"It almost sounds like you're saying caffeine is a *bad* thing," H.R. said with horror, clutching his triple latte to his chest possessively.

"It's a drug like any other," Caitlin said, shrugging. "You can get addicted to it. Using too much of it can lead to coma or even death."

H.R. shook his head, tsked, and glugged from his cup. "Fortunately, that clearly applies only to people from Earth 1."

"He'll be OK once he gets enough sleep," Caitlin said. She pondered for a moment. "Caffeine's a strong diuretic and can lead to dehydration. I should give him a saline IV. Why didn't I think of that before?"

"Look, can we cut to the chase?" Joe asked. "When can we expect him to wake up?"

"People who've been sleep-deprived can easily go a full day or more asleep before their natural rhythms wake them. An Australian hypnotist once kept someone asleep for something like eight days with no ill effects."

"You're saying he's not waking up anytime soon," H.R. said. "But when he does, don't you worry—I'll have a cup of wake-up juice waiting for him." He raised his coffee cup, which was as big as a salad bowl, and slurped ostentatiously.

"It's time for Plan B, then," Barry said. He hoisted up a complicated harness, its straps united by a solid-looking circular gadget roughly the size of the lightning bolt logo on his Flash costume.

"What's that?" Joe asked.

"My ticket to Earth 2. It's the tachyon harness that Cisco created, the one I used to explore the Multiverse before he started vibing. That's how I met Kara, I mean, Supergirl, remember?"

"She's the alien, the one who flies, right?" Joe asked. "Keeping track of you people is like living in a Pokémon cartoon."

Iris frowned. "Wasn't there a problem with the tachyon harness? You ended up on the wrong Earth and you almost couldn't get home."

"It'll be fine," Barry assured her.

"Yeah, we'll be OK," Wally chimed in.

Barry grinned. "You're not going."

"What?" Wally threw his hands up in the air. "I never get to go anywhere! Come on! I proved myself with Hocus Pocus, didn't I? Don't leave me on the sidelines! I can handle being a hero."

"I know you can," Barry told him. "That's why I'm trusting you to head up Team Flash and lead the Earthworm investigation while I'm gone. You've earned it."

Wally had the good graces to blush. "Oh." For once, he had nothing to say.

"What about your job, Bar?" Joe asked, concerned. "You want us running around after Earthworm while you go gallivanting off into the Multiverse . . . Shouldn't you maybe put a little time in with your union rep and work on persuading Captain Singh to keep you on board?"

Barry shook his head. His personal difficulties would have to take a backseat to the far more urgent problems before him. "No time for that right now. I have a couple more days until my hearing. That's a lifetime to a speedster. I'll deal with the CCPD after we've straightened out Hocus Pocus and figured out this whole Earthworm thing." He could tell that Joe wanted to say more, but cut him off. "My job means the world to me, but the world isn't going to be worth living in if Hocus Pocus comes back and starts mind-controlling people and turning trees into his own personal army again."

"I'm pretty sure we need a *Lord of the Rings* reference here," Caitlin said, "but I'm not sure how to do it. We really need Cisco to wake up!"

Everyone laughed. It was a good tension reliever. They'd just come through a rough week and thought they would have a break, but here they were, already knocked back on their heels, on the defensive.

Well, not for long.

* * *

Before he headed into the guts of the S.T.A.R. Labs particle accelerator, Barry grabbed Joe by the elbow and pulled him aside. He glanced around to make sure they were alone.

"Hey, look, Joe, I know what I said in there, but Wally's still a kid. And you're a cop. So . . ."

Joe chuckled deep in his throat. "You think I was gonna let my kid go off spelunking in the sewers alone? Without backup? C'mon—you grew up in my house. You know better than that."

Barry pulled Joe in for a hug. "I knew I could count on you. Keep everyone safe, Joe. I shouldn't be long."

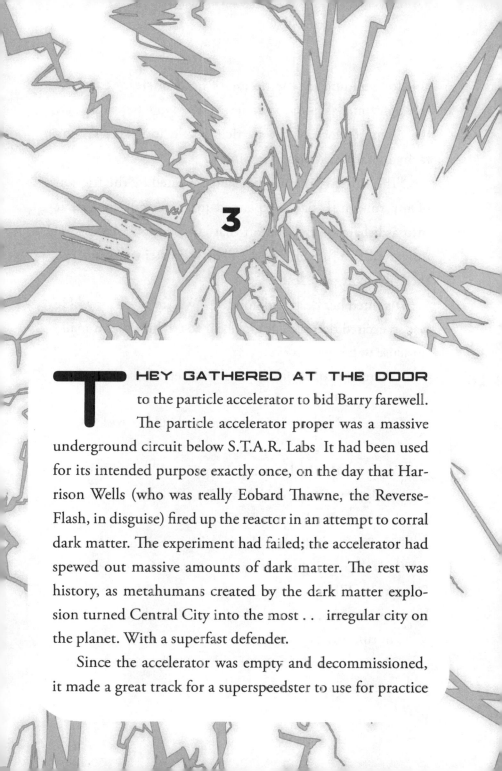

3

THEY GATHERED AT THE DOOR
to the particle accelerator to bid Barry farewell.
The particle accelerator proper was a massive
underground circuit below S.T.A.R. Labs. It had been used
for its intended purpose exactly once, on the day that Harrison Wells (who was really Eobard Thawne, the Reverse-
Flash, in disguise) fired up the reactor in an attempt to corral
dark matter. The experiment had failed; the accelerator had
spewed out massive amounts of dark matter. The rest was
history, as metahumans created by the dark matter explosion turned Central City into the most . . . irregular city on
the planet. With a superfast defender.

Since the accelerator was empty and decommissioned,
it made a great track for a superspeedster to use for practice

and for building up the necessary head of steam to travel through time, as he'd done a few times. Now he would run the circumference of the particle accelerator with Cisco's tachyon harness strapped to him.

"The harness takes in the energy created by the friction of my running," Barry explained to Iris, "and converts it into a disharmonic vibration that cuts me loose from this universe. It's a function of the Planck-Einstein relation and the Dirac constant, really."

Iris tilted her head and nodded. "Whatever you say." He was so excited that she couldn't bear to tell him that it made no sense to her whatsoever.

"There are equations," he told her earnestly. "I'll show them to you when I get back."

"Please do." She crossed her fingers behind her back. "Can't wait."

"You sure this is the smart thing to do?" Joe asked. "Do you really want to do this? Maybe Wally's right and we should just try harder to wake Cisco up."

"It's Earth 2," Barry said with a lilt in his voice that said *Chill out*. "Zoom's gone; it's perfectly safe. It's like going to Wisconsin. I'll zip over there, get the skinny on this"—he held up Hocus Pocus's wand—"and zip back here. It's not like I'm running over to Earth 666."

"There are only fifty-two Earths," Wally said, a bit more pedantically than necessary.

"I think it was a joke," Iris chided her brother.

Barry kissed her briefly, aware that Joe and the others were watching, then thought better of it and gave her a long, passionate kiss. Joe cleared his throat. Wally looked away. H.R. hooted and clacked his drumsticks together.

"So you won't forget me," Barry told her when they broke apart.

Iris pretended to fan herself. "Like *that*'s gonna happen!"

"Bye."

"Love you."

"Love you, too." Barry slipped his cowl over his face and made a last check of the tachyon harness strapped to his chest. All systems were go.

He set the tachyon harness's mechanism and then took off, zipping around the accelerator. Lightning crackled around him, coruscating in a whirl of flashing light and power. The tachyon harness began vibrating against his chest. The world around him started to become indistinct, to blur as though made of watercolors in a thunderstorm.

He ran faster. The particle accelerator had become a smear of gray, lit by the fiery sparks of his own personal electrical field as it spat lightning into the air.

An instant passed. Another. He made a thousand more circuits of the particle accelerator and then spied the opening breach, the pathway to Earth 2.

Without a second thought, he darted inside and felt the universe of Earth 1 slip away around him.

He should have waited.

He should have waited one more hour, which was how long it took for Cisco to wake up.

Just one more hour, and he would have spared himself so much.

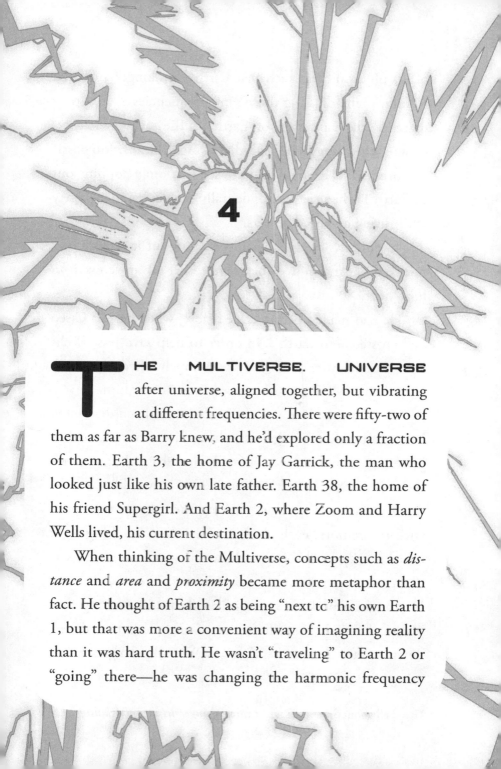

4

THE MULTIVERSE. UNIVERSE after universe, aligned together, but vibrating at different frequencies. There were fifty-two of them as far as Barry knew, and he'd explored only a fraction of them. Earth 3, the home of Jay Garrick, the man who looked just like his own late father. Earth 38, the home of his friend Supergirl. And Earth 2, where Zoom and Harry Wells lived, his current destination.

When thinking of the Multiverse, concepts such as *distance* and *area* and *proximity* became more metaphor than fact. He thought of Earth 2 as being "next to" his own Earth 1, but that was more a convenient way of imagining reality than it was hard truth. He wasn't "traveling" to Earth 2 or "going" there—he was changing the harmonic frequency of his physical form such that Earth 1 no longer appeared to him, then adjusting those same frequencies so that they matched the vibrations of Earth 2. The tachyon harness cohered the energy of his speed, making the transition possible; otherwise he would find himself randomly popping out of Earth 1 whenever he accidentally hit a certain frequency while using his speed powers.

Truthfully, it was easier just to think of it as "running next door to Earth 2." The science of it all made even *his* head hurt.

He had made this run once before, when he and Cisco had crossed into Earth 2 in order to help save Jesse Wells from Zoom. After that, he'd pretty much relied on Cisco's burgeoning "vibe" powers to open breaches for him.

The last time he'd run to Earth 2, he'd been distracted by a multitude of images assaulting him. They seemed to be mirages, but they were actually flickering glimpses into the other realities of the Multiverse. It was like switching TV channels quickly, clicking them by at top speed with the remote, each channel a universe, catching sight momentarily until you found the one you wanted and settled on it.

He caught a peek at Supergirl on Earth 38, soaring over National City, her cape fluttering in the breeze, then diving down toward a natural spring . . . Were those *tigers* swimming in there?*

*Read all about Supergirl's adventures in *Supergirl: Age of Atlantis!*

Then that image was swept aside and replaced with a boy with long blond hair wrestling with what appeared to be a bipedal lion.

The Multiverse is a weird place, he barely had time to think before that image, too, vanished. Now he beheld a woman in a purple tunic and tiara, gesturing toward a man whose face was dark and scarred. Then he saw a boy shouting to the sky as thunder clapped.

C'mon, Earth 2. Where's that frequency?

He tapped at the tachyon harness and glanced down. He was swathed in electricity and the furor of his own lightning, but somewhere amid all of that, he noticed a single spark, a jagged red bolt that leaped from the wand clutched in his right hand.

Oh no!

He'd been so captivated by the Multiversal montage playing out before him that he hadn't noticed that his pumping arms had brought the wand into contact with the tachyon harness. That red electrical discharge raced back and forth between the harness and the wand, becoming deeper and more violent looking by the second.

What do I do? What's this gonna do to me?

The Multiverse continued to swirl around him. A man with a glowing green ring on his hand. A rabbit in a cape and unitard. A man and woman smaller than mice, wearing red capes, running along what looked like the turret of an old World War II–era tank. A gleaming silver building floating in the air . . .

And then a glimpse, quick and almost missed, of Jay Garrick, the Flash of Earth 3, racing against a getaway car. Sunlight glinted off his winged Mercury helmet. Barry reached toward him and tried to cry out for help.

But the image whirled and spun away from him. A jolt ran up Barry's arm, the one holding the wand. Distracted for a moment, he lost his stride, his right foot coming down shallow. His pace juddered and he slued to one side.

An explosion of colors coursed around him, enveloped him. He was drowning in cyans, magentas, yellows, and blacks. He opened his mouth to scream, but there was no sound here; there was nothing to scream into.

The colors swallowed him whole, flashing before his eyes, pulsating in a pattern so fast that even the Flash could not keep track, and then he felt something solid beneath his feet and he slammed to a halt in the darkness, crashing headlong into *something*, and the darkness and the quiet became his entire world.

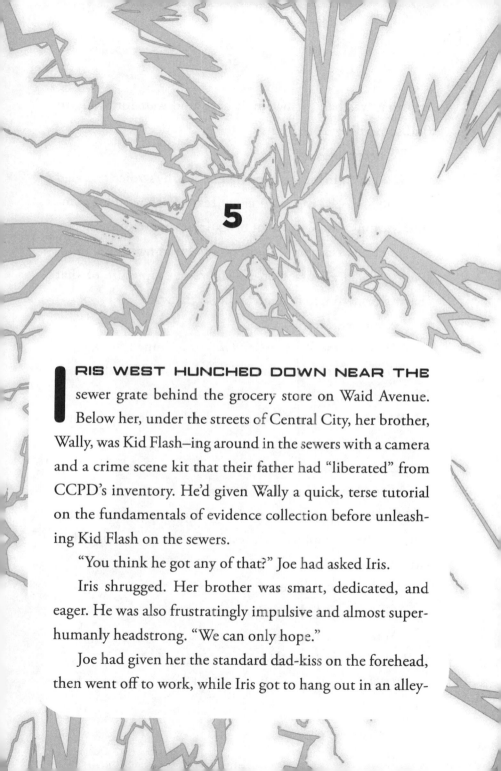

5

IRIS WEST HUNCHED DOWN NEAR THE
sewer grate behind the grocery store on Waid Avenue.
Below her, under the streets of Central City, her brother,
Wally, was Kid Flash–ing around in the sewers with a camera
and a crime scene kit that their father had "liberated" from
CCPD's inventory. He'd given Wally a quick, terse tutorial
on the fundamentals of evidence collection before unleashing Kid Flash on the sewers.

"You think he got any of that?" Joe had asked Iris.

Iris shrugged. Her brother was smart, dedicated, and
eager. He was also frustratingly impulsive and almost super-
humanly headstrong. "We can only hope."

Joe had given her the standard dad-kiss on the forehead,
then went off to work, while Iris got to hang out in an alley-

way that was bad for her high heels and wait for Wally to find something. Anything.

"Where are you?"

"Tough to maneuver down here." Wally's voice crackled over the S.T.A.R. Labs frequency Team Flash used for communications. There was a lot of static, owing to the concrete and steel between them. "Slow going. Heading for the room I told you all about before. Want to get a picture of that 'Earthworm' someone scratched into the wall."

"Got it. Be careful."

"They call me *Wallace Careful West* in some towns."

"You've never been out of Keystone and Central in your life. What towns?"

Wally's laugh was interspersed with static. "Got me. OK, I'm here. Hang on."

Iris sighed and looked at her watch impatiently. Her boyfriend and her brother could both move at superspeed. She'd long become accustomed to things happening *fast*, and her patience had atrophied as a result. The seconds dragged by interminably.

"Wally, you still there?"

"Getting the lighting right," he told her.

"You're not shooting pictures for a gallery opening," she said a little more irritably than she'd intended.

"Dad said to get the lighting right so that we can have

a record of the depth of the scratches." Wally sounded a bit wounded.

Smiling, Iris wished she could send her father a mental message: *He listened, Dad! Progress!*

"Take your time," she said.

"He'll be all right, you know." She didn't have to ask who he meant. Barry. Dashing off into the Multiverse like he was jogging around the corner for a bagel.

"Yeah, I know. I'm not worried."

"You're totally worried."

She grimaced and thought back to just a couple of hours earlier, at the pier. The boarded-up building that Barry swore had, just a few days before, housed the mysterious Madame Xanadu. For her to have been there and then for the place to suddenly appear abandoned for months . . . Well, you couldn't explain something like that with metahumanity and particle accelerator explosions. Was there a superpower that could make things old and disused? She didn't think so.

So either Madame Xanadu was legit magical . . . or Barry was going a little off his rocker. Both notions made her nervous and more than a little anxious.

"There's a lot to worry about," she told Wally.

"True. OK, got my pics. Gonna do some scouting."

"Be . . ." She caught herself before she could say *careful* again. ". . . effective."

"They call me *Wallace Effective West* in some towns."

She couldn't help it; she exploded with laughter there in the dirty alleyway. Her cell phone chirped at that moment and she glanced down at it.

"Wally, get back up here. Now."

"I was just getting started!"

"Cisco's awake!"

"Explain this to me again!" Cisco demanded. "And someone get this thing out of me!" He flapped one arm, which was tethered to an IV drip. He was standing, woozy and clutching the IV pole, next to the bed where he'd slept for over a day. Iris, Wally, H.R., and Caitlin stood around him, none of them willing to risk stepping within range of his flailing arm. Cisco was still figuring out his vibe powers, after all, and didn't have perfect control yet. Who knew what he might accidentally do when emotionally revved up?

"Barry went to Earth 2 to get Harry's help with the magic wand," Caitlin said. She did a double take. "Wow. That is a sentence I never thought I would utter. Actually, I never thought *anyone* would ever utter it."

Cisco groaned. "The tachyon harness is still *experimental*. You should have waited for me." He pressed two fingers to his temple.

"What are you vibing?" Wally asked.

"Nothing." Cisco moaned just the slightest bit. "My head is killing me, that's all."

"Caffeine withdrawal," Caitlin said primly.

"Francisco!" H.R. proffered a steaming mug. "Hair of the dog, my compadre!"

Caitlin slapped H.R.'s wrist, which jostled the cup. Hot coffee dripped onto the floor as H.R. cried out in pitiable horror. "No. No more caffeine for him. Leave the IV in, Cisco. The fluids will help balance you out and mitigate the rebound headache."

Cisco grudgingly agreed and sat down on the bed. "So you just let Barry go running off into the Multiverse without me. You guys suck."

"You were asleep," Iris reminded him. "And we need to figure out what's next for Hocus Pocus."

"Or Abra Kadabra," Wally pointed out. "He called himself that at the end, remember?"

At the words *Abra Kadabra*, Cisco's already pained expression became even more complicated.

"I'll add some magnesium sulfate to your IV," said Caitlin. "That should help your headache."

"No, no." Cisco waved her away. "Just . . . help me up. I need to get to my workshop."

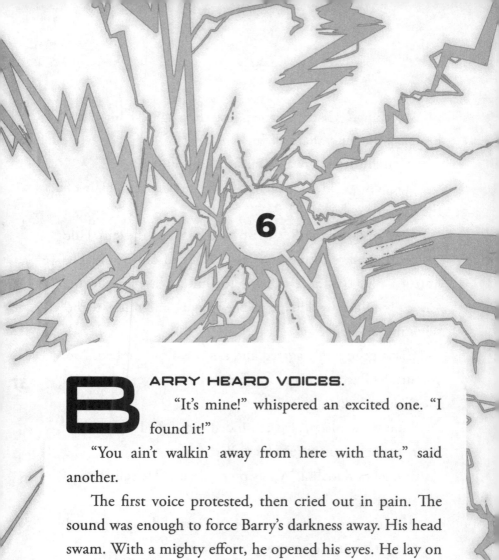

6

BARRY HEARD VOICES.

"It's mine!" whispered an excited one. "I found it!"

"You ain't walkin' away from here with that," said another.

The first voice protested, then cried out in pain. The sound was enough to force Barry's darkness away. His head swam. With a mighty effort, he opened his eyes. He lay on dirty concrete. Every bone and every muscle in his body ached, throbbing with unforgiving pain. A groan escaped from his lips, and the two voices came back to him.

"Holy! You see that? It's *him*!" The first, excited voice.

"Don't be an idiot," said the second voice. "That's the wrong costume."

Barry swiveled his head to his right. Somehow, he must have instinctively navigated his way to his destination, for he lay in an alleyway on Earth 2, trash and debris strewn around him. Hissing in a tortured breath, Barry twisted his body in the direction of the voices. About twenty yards away, two figures stood facing him, their features blurry and indistinct. He blinked his eyes and things cleared a little bit, but not much.

"He's awake!" the first voice cried.

"Good for him." The second voice belonged to someone much taller and broader. A gruff, no-nonsense voice. As Barry watched, the bigger man grabbed something from the smaller man.

"Give it back!"

He blinked again, feverishly trying to clear his vision, and realized what it was.

The wand!

"Give . . ." Barry croaked. "Give it—"

"Max speed!" Voice Two shoved Voice One, sending the smaller man careening into a haphazardly stacked pile of boxes and old wooden beams. The pile shook and quaked, then collapsed on top of the smaller man, trapping him beneath.

Barry pushed himself to his knees, ready to leap up and give chase. An eddy of dizziness swirled around him, and he almost collapsed again, his chest heaving.

By the time he collected himself and could stand without feeling as though he would throw up his internal organs, the bigger man, the one with Hocus Pocus's wand, was halfway down the alley. Barry prepared to give chase but out of the corner of his eye noticed the smaller man, who was now pinned beneath a mountain of debris. The man cried out in pain, and Barry realized that a sharp shard of wood had pierced him through the leg. Blood ran down his pants and pooled on the ground.

He could give chase to the guy with the wand, or he could help the injured one.

That was no choice at all.

He sped to the side of the injured man. "Hang on," he said. "I've got this."

Moving at superspeed, he removed the boxes and wood beams that had collapsed, stacking them against the wall on the opposite side of the alley. In a few seconds, he had the man completely uncovered.

The man stared at him with a frozen expression and unrelenting terror in his eyes.

"You're going to be OK," Barry promised. "I can get this out."

He would just touch one end of the shard and vibrate, pulling it free instantly. Then he'd quickly tie a bandage around the man's leg before any more blood could flow.

Then maybe a quick run to the closest hospital. Easy.

But . . .

"Don't hurt me!" The man pulled his legs back, curling them against his chest and wincing in pain. "Don't kill me!"

"What? I'm not going to—"

"Don't hurt me! Please!"

Taken aback, Barry did nothing as the man braced himself against the wall and got to his feet. He was clearly in pain as he put weight on the injured leg, but his absolute terror won out.

Barry reached out to help him stand, but the man screamed a high, keening scream and slapped Barry's hand away. Then, still bawling at the top of his lungs, he limp-ran down the alley as fast as he could.

Which, truthfully, was not very fast. Barry could have easily caught up with him and almost did, but then he realized what had happened.

Zoom, he thought. *The last speedster the people of Earth 2 saw was Zoom. They're terrified of anyone with speed.*

He frowned. This wasn't ideal, but overcoming Earth 2's fear of speed would have to wait for another time. He'd lost the wand. He was in a dirty alleyway. Fortunately, the urban geography of Central City on Earth 2 was pretty similar to that of Earth 1. He recognized the bulge of Julius Stadium in the distance, which meant that he wasn't far from S.T.A.R.

Labs. If he knew Harry, the man would be in his office or his lab, no matter the hour. Maybe Harry could help him figure out a way to track the wand. It had to have unique properties due to its nanite generator, right? They could figure *something* out . . .

He was still shaky on his feet. Whatever he'd done to himself while traveling between realities, it wasn't something that could be fixed with a few deep breaths and knee bends, both of which he'd tried already. He paced the alley for a few moments, pausing to stretch and lean, shaking the soreness from his muscles. Then he took off, tearing down the street toward S.T.A.R. Labs. Harry and Jesse would be shocked to see him. It would be good to see them again, and he wished he could make the time to just enjoy their company, but the clock was ticking—he needed to get back on Hocus Pocus's trail.

And Earthworm . . .

Oh, yeah—and he needed to figure out how to keep his job, too. Sheesh. Way too much to do.

He was so lost in his own thoughts that he nearly crashed headlong into a wall that shouldn't have been there. He skidded to a halt just in time, kicking up a plume of dust and smoke in his wake.

The wall was made of concrete blocks stacked more than thirty feet high. It stretched across Fox Boulevard, over the sidewalks on either side, right up to the buildings left and right, forming an impenetrable barricade. At the top of the wall, he spotted shiny curls of concertina wire, glimmering in the light from the streetlamps along the boulevard. Poking up over the deadly razor wire, one of the towers of the S.T.A.R. Labs complex stood in stark relief against the blackening sky.

"Step back, peon!" a voice sounded out, amplified by a PA system. "You're within the No-Go Zone!"

Barry looked up and around for the source of the voice. Nothing. At his feet, he noticed he was standing on a painted series of red crosshatches that stretched out to the wall and then back behind him a good thirty or forty feet.

He held his hands in the air to show he meant no harm. "I'm looking for Harrison Wells!" he called out.

"Step. Back!" The voice sounded more insistent now. "You know the penalty for being in the No-Go Zone!"

Barry turned in a slow circle, looking up. He still couldn't see where the voice was coming from. "Where's Harrison Wells? Tell him the Flash—"

"Harrison Wells is dead!" the voice boomed. "And so are you!"

Gunshots rang out.

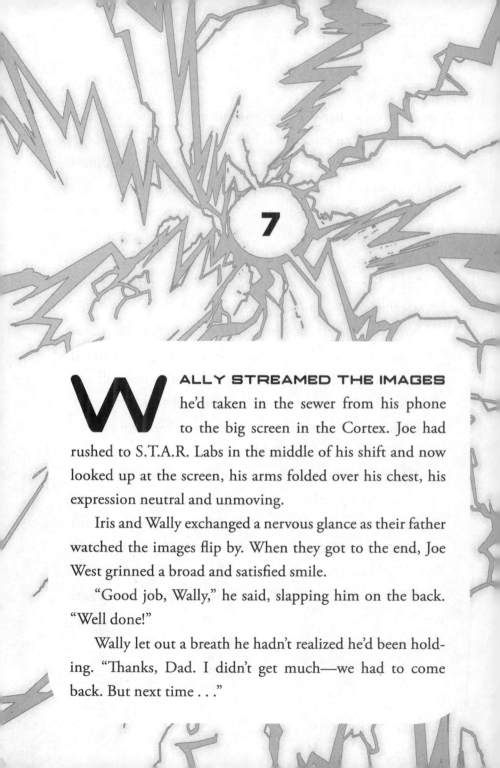

7

WALLY STREAMED THE IMAGES he'd taken in the sewer from his phone to the big screen in the Cortex. Joe had rushed to S.T.A.R. Labs in the middle of his shift and now looked up at the screen, his arms folded over his chest, his expression neutral and unmoving.

Iris and Wally exchanged a nervous glance as their father watched the images flip by. When they got to the end, Joe West grinned a broad and satisfied smile.

"Good job, Wally," he said, slapping him on the back. "Well done!"

Wally let out a breath he hadn't realized he'd been holding. "Thanks, Dad. I didn't get much—we had to come back. But next time . . ."

"Don't sell yourself short," Iris told him.

Bouncing on his toes, Wally slapped his hands together. "I just want to get this guy, you know? Preferably before Barry gets back."

Joe's expression became thoughtful as he put a hand on Wally's shoulder to slow him down. "You don't have to prove anything to Barry, son. He knows what you're capable of."

Iris nodded in agreement. She hated to see her brother so worked up over demonstrating his worth. He was a great brother, a great person, a great hero. "No one thinks you can't get this done, Wally."

"It's not that," Wally said earnestly. "I'm not trying to prove myself or anything. It's just that . . . Barry has so much on his plate right now. He's got Hocus Pocus and he's got this big hearing coming up to see if he keeps his job. I just want to take something away. Lighten his load a little. You know?"

Now it was Joe's turn to exchange a glance with Iris. His chest felt too small for the pride pumping through his heart at that moment. "Wally, man . . ." He pulled his son in for a hug. "You impress the heck outta me, kid." He kissed the top of Wally's head.

"Dad!" Wally complained, pulling away. "Too much parental affection. A little goes a long way."

Joe chuckled. "All right then. Let's do like Wally said.

Let's take some things off Barry's plate. Where do we start?"

Iris thought for a moment. "I'll check with city records and the *Picture News* files to see if there are any references to Earthworm."

Joe nodded. "And I'll do like Barry suggested the other day and look for unsolved cases with missing organs from the last year or so. See if anything pops."

"And I'll—"

"Get to school," Joe interrupted Wally. "Your classes are about to begin."

"But Dad—!"

Joe raised an eyebrow and gave Wally his best cop glare. Wally huffed a sigh of annoyance and nodded, then sped off to class.

"He's too easy sometimes," Joe said, chuckling.

"He didn't grow up with you," Iris pointed out. "He doesn't know what a pussycat you are in real life. He'll figure it out."

Joe considered. "Until then, I'm gonna enjoy having *one* kid who actually listens to me!"

Elsewhere in the S.T.A.R. Labs complex, Cisco Ramon stared at the pile of clothes and felt a tremble deep inside.

Just clothes, he told himself. *It's just some dude's clothes.*

But in this case, *some dude* was none other than Hocus

Pocus. Who had uttered the words *Abra Kadabra.* Which for some reason had filled Cisco with dread.

Hocus Pocus. Abra Kadabra. Silly "magic words" that did and meant nothing. And yet . . .

When Barry had told them all that Hocus Pocus had a master named Abra Kadabra, Cisco had felt, for a fleeting instant, the tingle of a vibe. But this one hadn't been like his usual vibes. He'd gotten somewhat used to them, as much as one can get used to having the floor drop out from under them. But this one . . .

It had been familiar and unfamiliar at the same time. Like staring through a window at a beautiful meadow, only to realize that you are, in fact, looking at a startlingly lifelike painting.

Abra Kadabra. Say the magic word and . . . what happens?

He'd glimpsed . . . something. His vibe visions were usually off-kilter and imperfect, clotted with static and filtered through odd colors. But this one had been more problematic than usual. He'd been unable to focus his attention on anything for any appreciable amount of time, smash-cutting from one image to another, a dozen of them in less than a second. Nothing had stuck; nothing made an impression.

But he'd had such a bad feeling. A bad *vibe*, if that weren't a pun even he was too classy to use.

Those words had triggered images, yes, but more important than the images, they'd triggered a sense of pure *wrong*.

He'd felt something broken and jagged, like a splintered tree trunk after a lightning strike. Something so ineffably incorrect and corrupt that his stomach lurched and his throat closed up.

And then he'd forced it to the back of his mind, like a bad nightmare on waking, and gone on with the business of helping Barry defeat the villain du jour.

But now was the time to go back into the nightmare. To figure it out. To conquer it.

Barry had taken the wand to Earth 2, but he'd left behind Hocus Pocus's clothes, and now all Cisco had to do was touch them. Just touch them. Vibe off of them.

Come on.

No big deal.

Just reach out. Extend your arm, your hand. Your fingers.

Just . . .

. . . touch . . .

. . . them . . .

He did. He brushed his fingertips along the white cloth—and the vibe smashed into him like a hard, angry wave at high tide. No chance to ease into it. No opportunity to steel himself. It was just *there*, singing its harmonies all around him, pulsating in his skull like a too-loud rock concert. He thought of the time his older brother, Dante, had sneaked him out of the house to hitch a ride to Star City to see the Ramones. Cisco was only seven years old, but he and Dante loved the band, and this was their farewell tour. It was one of the few times Dante had treated him like a person, not like a tether, and he'd loved it, even though the loudness of the music had taken over his own heartbeat, commandeered his body, sent him shaking and quaking. They'd gotten in *soooo* much trouble, but it had been worth it.

Good memory. Good time. He clung to it as the vibe battered him, relentless, unstoppable. His vision went red, then black, then a hue of gold he'd never seen before. The room at S.T.A.R. Labs faded from view, the walls throbbing into infinity, vanishing, the floor dropping away. He clung to the memory of that time with Dante, using it to root him to his spot, clenching his fingers now into the cloth, like an anchor, as though it would stop him from spinning off into the infinite wastelands of the universe that now whirled around him.

And then the images came. Rapid-fire, one disappearing as soon as it appeared, melting right into the next one, which also vanished so quickly he couldn't make them out.

Or could he?

Joe was running down the hall. At S.T.A.R. Labs? Maybe. Couldn't be sure.

Gun. *Big* gun. Bristling with tech. Looked like something Cisco himself might have designed and built.

He gritted his teeth and focused all of his concentration on the vibe. It was like leaning into a hurricane, with bits of trash and rain whipping past in the high, howling winds. Nevertheless, he pushed forward, slowing down the visions by sheer force of will.

A man . . .

A man. In the Pipeline. Cisco had never seen him before. Dressed in all black, jacket and slacks, shirt and tie, like a man about to go out on the town. Steel-gray hair, immaculately sculpted into a wave. Goatee. Snotty, supercilious sneer.

Joe again, running. Shooting that big gun at something . . .

What? What was he seeing? The future?

The man in black strode confidently into a S.T.A.R. Labs elevator. He had the air of a man who is invulnerable, someone who cannot be defeated or even hurt.

Cisco cried out as the vibe shuddered and shook all around him. His vision flickered in sickly greens and harsh yellows. He had the distinct sense that something was *breaking*, that something very strong, but very fragile, had been manhandled beyond its limits. The supports beneath him were giving way, and he thought that if he persisted, he might become lost in this vibe forever, wandering its broken, blinking landscape, looking for the impossible way home.

And then something real intruded on the vibe. A voice

cried out, as if from a great distance. It felt familiar to him, as did the touch on his arm.

Suddenly the vibe disappeared. It did not fade away or gradually diminish—one moment it was *there*, it was *all*, and in the next instant, it was *gone*.

Caitlin stood before him, breathing hard. In her hands, she held Hocus Pocus's clothes, which she'd clearly torn from Cisco's grasp with great effort.

"Caitlin?" His voice came to him on a far-off wave. It sounded distant and hollow.

"Are you OK?" she asked, catching her breath. "You were standing so still . . . Just standing there like a statue, but you were making this weird humming sound and you didn't respond to me when I tried to talk to you, so I . . ." She held up the clothing and shrugged.

"It's OK," he told her. He put his hands over his eyes for a moment, closing them tight, trying to sort through what he'd seen. "None of it made any sense. It was *now*. I know that. I was seeing now, but none of it is actually happening. It's like . . . It's like . . ." He cast about for a metaphor that could explain the sensation to her, but came up empty. Nothing could possibly explain the feeling he'd had while in the vibe, the feeling that he was witnessing something immediate and, at the same time, impossible. Something occurring, but also that could never, ever occur.

"Are you all right?" she asked gently, and touched him on the shoulder. "You've been pushing yourself so hard. You need to take care of yourself."

"I'm OK," he promised her. "I'm really, really OK. It's just a lot going on right now. That's all." He still had his hands over his eyes, and he felt something wet on his face. He laughed at himself and lowered his hands. "And now I'm crying. Great."

"Cisco!" Caitlin's voice was alarmed. "Those aren't tears! That's blood!"

Looking at his fingertips, sure enough he saw that they glimmered red.

"Well, that can't be good," he said.

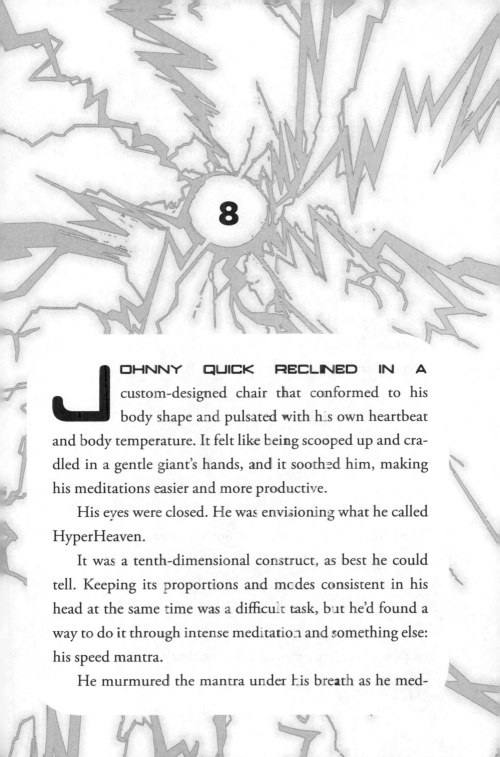

8

JOHNNY QUICK RECLINED IN A custom-designed chair that conformed to his body shape and pulsated with his own heartbeat and body temperature. It felt like being scooped up and cradled in a gentle giant's hands, and it soothed him, making his meditations easier and more productive.

His eyes were closed. He was envisioning what he called HyperHeaven.

It was a tenth-dimensional construct, as best he could tell. Keeping its proportions and modes consistent in his head at the same time was a difficult task, but he'd found a way to do it through intense meditation and something else: his speed mantra.

He murmured the mantra under his breath as he meditated. The chair began to shake as his body vibrated with intense superspeed. The world blurred. He was both in control and out of control at the same time, on the precipice of understanding the power that had been granted to him by fate and by chance.

The power that had helped reshape the world.

He thought he saw something. Just on the edge of reality. Sometimes, when he moved fast enough and at just the right frequency, the world seemed to fade into a blur, and something *else* hovered there, right on the edge of his perceptions. It might be another world. It might be the path to HyperHeaven. He couldn't be sure.

But he wanted to know.

He *would* know.

He had power, yes, but he needed more. If he was to hold off the others and keep them from—

"Sir?"

Quick gritted his teeth in anger at the interruption. There was a statue standing before him. Just another stupid statue that could talk and walk, when he allowed it.

That's how he thought of them. The slow ones. The non-gifted. They were statues to him. He could move amongst them at hyper speed, invisible to their statue senses, undetectable. They only moved when he deigned to slow down, when he permitted it.

He could walk through their walls, spy on them, take what was theirs, take *them*.

Pathetic statues. Sometimes he thought . . .

He sighed. Business to attend to.

He sat up in the chair, not bothering to slow his speed. He was a man-shaped blur to the statue, who gulped in fear before speaking.

"Sir, I'm sorry for interrupting your meditation."

"Speak." He liked the sound his voice made when he vibrated it just so. A throaty, devastatingly intimidating basso profundo. It made the statues quake in their boots, as this one did now.

"Sir, the western No-Go Zone was breached. Security gave the standard warnings."

"And?"

"And the intruder did not obey."

Quick flexed the fingers of his right hand, then clenched them into a fist. "And so was immediately shot dead, per my orders. Why are you bothering me to tell me this?"

"Sir, that's just it." The statue was trembling now, in fear for its life. As it should be. "Security immediately opened fire, in harmony with your standing orders."

Quick thought for a moment. One of *his* moments—to the statue, it was a flickering of an eyelash. "Are you going to tell me that they *missed*?" Johnny didn't know whether to be enraged or amused. In all the years since he'd taken over Central City and turned it into his personal demesne, his troops had never failed him. They knew the penalty for failure was worse than death: exile into the lands beyond Central City and the merciless fates that awaited there. The idea that his guards would miss an intruder was laughable.

So he chose amusement. He chuckled. The statue should have relaxed at his reaction, but did not.

"Sir, they missed, yes, but only because the intruder ran."

Johnny laughed even louder. What a ridiculous excuse! His laughter took on a sinister air; he gloried in what he would do to those who'd failed him. Exile was too good for those who would attempt to save themselves on such a pathetic, risible pretext. He would shake their very atoms into mist for this.

"Ran? They're equipped with the finest assault weapon technology in the world, and they couldn't hit some scampering fool who—"

And the statue, taking its life in its own hands, dared to interrupt: "Sir, he ran like you do. He ran *fast*."

Johnny stopped laughing. Now it wasn't funny anymore.

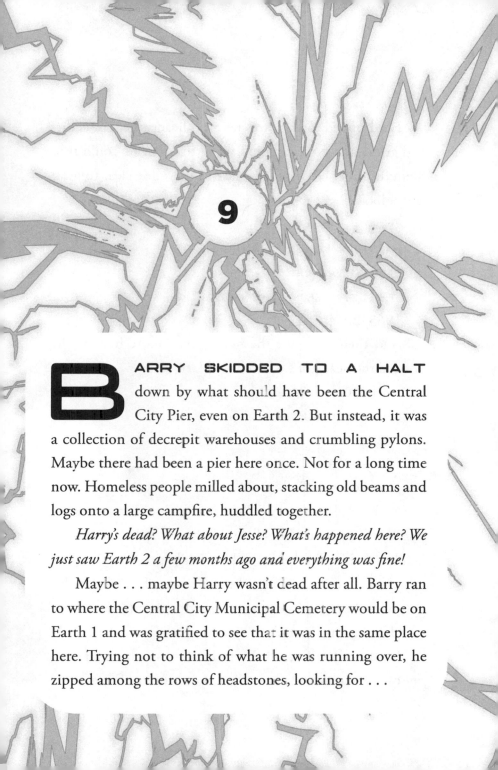

9

BARRY SKIDDED TO A HALT down by what should have been the Central City Pier, even on Earth 2. But instead, it was a collection of decrepit warehouses and crumbling pylons. Maybe there had been a pier here once. Not for a long time now. Homeless people milled about, stacking old beams and logs onto a large campfire, huddled together.

Harry's dead? What about Jesse? What's happened here? We just saw Earth 2 a few months ago and everything was fine!

Maybe . . . maybe Harry wasn't dead after all. Barry ran to where the Central City Municipal Cemetery would be on Earth 1 and was gratified to see that it was in the same place here. Trying not to think of what he was running over, he zipped among the rows of headstones, looking for . . .

No. No. Oh no . . .

He dropped to his knees before a headstone. Some dirt and grime and pollen clotted the letters, but he could read them just fine. He wiped the face of the stone clear to get a better look.

Yes.

HARRISON WELLS

BELOVED FATHER

"THE UNIVERSE IS LIT BY KNOWLEDGE"

1963–2014

And then, to make the horror even more horrific, he noticed the headstone adjacent to Harry's.

JESSE CHAMBERS WELLS

BELOVED DAUGHTER

"WE GO FASTER TO THE FUTURE"

1996–2014

Jesse, too. Oh God.

Shaky and sick, he reached out for the headstones to stabilize himself, lest he collapse to the ground and lie there, helpless and lost in the dirt of his friends' graves.

They were both gone. The grief was like a fist in his gut, like a heavy, spiked mace crushed against his heart. He couldn't breathe. He didn't *want* to breathe.

He didn't understand. Everything on Earth 2 had been *fine* once Zoom was defeated. It had only been a few months since he and the rest of Team Flash had bade Harry and Jesse farewell from S.T.A.R. Labs. Cisco had opened a breach, and then the two of them had leaped in with Jay Garrick, the Earth 3 Flash, to go home.

What had happened in those months? What had gone so wrong on Earth 2?

"I'm so sorry," he whispered. "I'm so sorry I wasn't here for you. I failed you. I'm so, so sorry."

He rested his forehead against Harry's tombstone. Deep down, he knew that he should be up, should be active. He should be doing something. Searching the city for clues as to what had happened. Tracking down Hocus Pocus's wand. Something. *Anything*. But the sheer palpability of his anguish, the physical hurt of the loss, made it impossible for him to move.

He'd lost his parents, and some part of him had thought that such a blow would inoculate him against lesser woes. After such pain, how could anything else ever seem to hurt again? And yet when Eddie Thawne—Eobard Thawne's ancestor and Barry's friend—had killed himself to save the universe, Barry had felt pain. When Ronnie Raymond had disappeared into the singularity, he'd grieved. And now here he was again, witness to more death—needless, pointless death—and he suffered as though new to it, as though born just now into the pain of the world.

He thought of the Time Wraiths that had followed him through the time stream and then had abducted Zoom into the Speed Force. They were harbingers of death, and he'd looked into their eyes and survived. But not everyone was so lucky. Barry ran fast, but no one could outrun death.

Apparently he could dodge it for a while, though. While it took everyone around him.

Sitting back on his haunches, he stared at the two headstones. He should leave. He couldn't just stay here. But where could he go? Where *should* he go?

As he pondered that, something caught his attention, something that, he realized, had been nagging at the back of his mind since he'd first laid eyes on the graves.

Something was wrong.

The names were right. The quotations sounded exactly like Harry and Jesse. It was something else.

The dates, he realized. They made no sense.

According to the dates on the tombstones, Harry and Jesse had died a few years ago. Right after the particle accelerator explosion, actually. But that was impossible. He'd seen them recently. They *couldn't* have died back then.

Unless . . .

His jaw dropped as he suddenly realized what was wrong. *I'm not on Earth 2!*

He'd just assumed that because he was *headed* to Earth 2, that was where he'd ended up. But that wasn't the case. He was somewhere else entirely. Thrown off his path by the sparking reaction between Hocus Pocus's wand and the tachyon harness.

And he had no idea where he'd been thrown. It's not like there was a guidebook to the Multiverse out there. If there were, he would pay an awful lot for a copy. It would make his life so much easier.

He stood up and paced, thinking, so absorbed that it no longer bothered him that he was walking over the dead. How could he figure out where he was? He'd stumbled onto the existence of the Multiverse purely by accident, learning of Earth 2, which then led to the discovery of Earth 3. And then there was the time he'd met Supergirl, when the malfunctioning tachyon harness had brought him to Earth 38. And he knew there were fifty-two universes, because fifty-two breaches had opened, each with its own vibrational signature. Beyond that, though . . .

He remembered seeing Jay and then taking a few more steps.

Well, Jay lived on Earth 3, and this Earth was somewhere beyond that. Call it three raised to its own power: three to the third. Twenty-seven. So until someone actually wrote that guidebook to the Multiverse and said otherwise, he would think of this particular dimension as Earth 27.

With a deep breath, he did something he should have done before: He looked down at the tachyon harness. It didn't look good. There were scorch marks all along its circumference. Barry stripped it off and laid it on the ground before him. He knelt down and poked at it, prying off its access door to peer into Cisco's meticulously designed electronic innards. He couldn't make head or tail of it, but he knew one thing for sure:

The tachyon harness was busted.

Well, that's it. I'm never using this thing again.

He laughed ruefully at himself. Sour grapes.

OK, then, I have two problems. One: Find the wand. Two: Find a way home.

He considered. Who was he kidding? *Three* problems.

Three: Figure out what went so wrong here. He couldn't just see Harry's and Jesse's doppelgängers dead and not try to learn why.

A sudden chill ran up his spine, bearing a hideous thought that he could not ignore, no matter how hard he tried. At superspeed, he performed the gruesome chore of checking the entire graveyard.

Cisco Ramon. Caitlin Snow. Joseph West. Iris West. All buried here as well, their deaths coming on the same day as this Earth's Harry and Jesse. Killed in the particle accelerator explosion or maybe from lingering aftereffects.

Gone.

All gone.

Barry bit his lower lip hard enough to draw blood. Who was going to help him now?

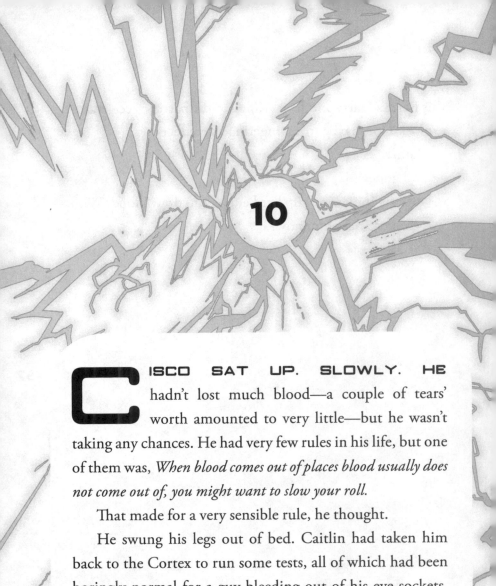

10

CISCO SAT UP. SLOWLY. HE hadn't lost much blood—a couple of tears' worth amounted to very little—but he wasn't taking any chances. He had very few rules in his life, but one of them was, *When blood comes out of places blood usually does not come out of, you might want to slow your roll.*

That made for a very sensible rule, he thought.

He swung his legs out of bed. Caitlin had taken him back to the Cortex to run some tests, all of which had been boringly normal for a guy bleeding out of his eye sockets. She'd had him lie down to rest; he'd protested and then fallen asleep anyway.

He was getting a little tired of waking up in the medical bay. It was old hat at this point.

Old hat made him think of a magician's hat, made him think of Hocus Pocus, made him think of Ab—

Don't. He almost said the word out loud, just to reinforce it for himself. *Don't say his name and don't even think it. Not now. Not until you can be sure you can figure this out. Treat this guy like Volde—He Who Shall Not Be Named.*

He stepped out into the Cortex. Caitlin was there alone and looked at him with a mix of professional concern and unprofessional pity.

"Don't," he told her. "Don't go all McCoy on me, Spock. I'm fine."

"You have a strange definition of *fine*," she told him.

"We have strange definitions for *everything* ever since the particle accelerator blew."

"Good point. Want to talk about what happened in your vibe?"

Cisco threw himself into a chair with a groan. "If I could articulate it at all, I'd talk about it nonstop. But I don't even know where to begin. I'm starting to feel useless."

Caitlin huffed laughter. "Useless? You built the machine that freed Barry from Hocus Pocus!"

"Yeah, well, what have I done for you lately?"

She stood and came over to him, hunkering down by his chair and putting a hand on his arm. "Believe it or not, Cisco, we love you for *you*, not for what you can do for us."

He snorted. Mostly because he believed her and it made him uncomfortable to be so real.

"But if you're really itching to do something, maybe forget about Hocus Pocus and think about what's taking Barry so long."

Cisco sat upright, knocking Caitlin's hand off of him. "He's not *back* yet? He's still gone?"

"Well—"

"I'm gonna go get him. I told you all that the harness wasn't ready for prime time. He's probably stuck on Earth 2."

He was out of the Cortex and running down the hall to the Breach Room before Caitlin could even yell, "Be careful!" but he heard it echoing down the corridor nonetheless.

Cisco focused on the air before him, seeking the tear in the fabric of reality.

Theoretically, he could "vibe" a breach anywhere in the world, but the Breach Room, deep in the bowels of S.T.A.R. Labs, was especially conducive to doing so. Many breaches had opened there during their extended fight against Zoom; the walls between dimensions seemed thinner and more porous in that space. In his still-shaky condition, he needed all the advantages he could stack on his side.

He concentrated, holding a hand out before him. He was reasonably certain that the gesture was unnecessary, but it helped sharpen his thinking and center his power.

After a few moments, the air before him began to ripple like water, an upright pond disturbed by a stone. He pushed with his mind, and the ripples doubled upon themselves. At the center of the concentric circles, a glimmer of light.

Earth 2.

Cisco stepped through the breach, and then it was as though he'd never been in the Breach Room, which sat dim and empty.

The lighting on Earth 2 always threw him for a loop when he first came through. There was something odd about the sunlight—everything outside had a strange amber hue to it. Cisco had always meant to ask Harry or Jesse why this was so. Was there some sort of atmospheric phenomenon that blocked certain light wavelengths? Shading his eyes with a hand, he gazed up at the sky. Blue sky. Clouds. Nothing obvious.

Oh well. A mystery for another time.

He'd vibed onto Earth 2 just outside S.T.A.R. Labs, so he wandered inside and approached the reception desk.

"Hi there!" he said to the woman seated there. "I'm here to see Harry."

She arched an annoyed eyebrow.

"Harrison Wells, I mean." He gifted her with his most resplendent smile.

She looked him up and down, taking in his battered Nikes, his baggy jeans, his vintage Atari T-shirt. "Do you have an appointment?" she asked in a tone of voice that told him she already knew the answer.

"He'll want to see me," he said confidently. "Tell him Cisco Ramon is here."

At the sound of his name, the receptionist's face went tight. Before he knew what was happening, alarms screeched, civilians ran for cover, and guards who seemed to be armed in preparation for Doomsday had surrounded him. Their rifles were very impressive—plasma bottles attached to electromagnetic launch tubes with augmented-reality sighting mechanisms. Nice stuff, if it wasn't pointed at you.

"Don't even move!" a guard shouted.

"Hands in the air!" another commanded.

"Uh, those are two contradictory orders!" Cisco said, panicked.

"Stop smart-mouthing and put your hands in the air!"

Cisco did as he was told.

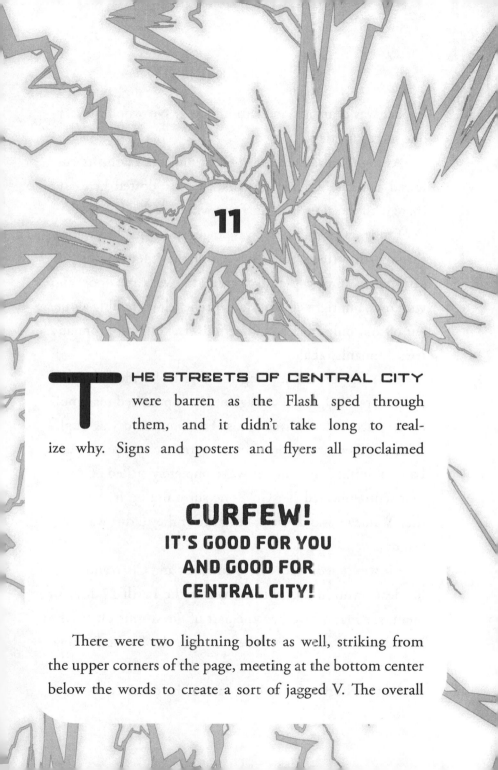

11

THE STREETS OF CENTRAL CITY were barren as the Flash sped through them, and it didn't take long to realize why. Signs and posters and flyers all proclaimed

CURFEW!
IT'S GOOD FOR YOU
AND GOOD FOR
CENTRAL CITY!

There were two lightning bolts as well, striking from the upper corners of the page, meeting at the bottom center below the words to create a sort of jagged V. The overall impact was dramatic and intimidating. No wonder everyone stayed inside.

As night closed around the city and the Flash, its curfewed citizens huddled indoors, the city dotted here and there with the glow of lights from windows.

Empty, Central City was a ghost town. Trash blew through the streets and clustered at the intersections. He knew there were people alive behind the walls and doors and windows, but right at that moment, he felt incredibly alone, cut off not only from his home universe, but also from any basic humanity at all.

Keeping himself moving too fast to be identified, he checked out S.T.A.R. Labs again. His superspeed reconnoiter revealed that the wall across Fox Boulevard was duplicated at other intersections on the perimeter of the S.T.A.R. Labs building. The complex was completely walled off, with that red-delineated No-Go Zone surrounding it even further. Whoever was in there, he or she or they didn't want any visitors.

He wondered: With Harry and Jesse and Cisco and Caitlin dead, who lurked within? Was it the Earth 27 Martin Stein, the man who'd become part of Firestorm? Or maybe Ronnie Raymond? Or maybe someone else he didn't know yet?

With a burst of speed, he ran to the outskirts of town

and found more walls at every point of ingress or egress. The on-ramps and off-ramps to the highway were barricaded, as were the local access roads. He ran up the side of a nearby building. It was only fifteen stories high, but its rooftop gave him a vantage point from which he could look over the walls around the city.

Beyond Central City was a no-man's-land of blasted, scorched earth in a ring extending out ten or fifteen miles. The highway was a ramshackle mess, a broken belt of crumbling asphalt. Farther out, he saw overgrowth and trees, as though nature had gone cruel and lusted to reclaim its territory. From what he could tell, it was doing a pretty good job.

Also on the other side of the wall, he noticed several vehicles that seemed to glide a few feet above the ground, milling about, moving in patterns that he soon realized were patrols. Each vehicle was the size of a small car, coated with a dull finish that seemed to deflect light, giving the vehicles the appearance of armored beetles. They moved like floating hippos and were emblazoned with the same lightning V he'd noted on the curfew signs.

Unconsciously, he touched the symbol on his chest. He didn't like seeing it corrupted. It gave him a dull, achy feeling in his gut.

Are they keeping people out or keeping them in? he wondered.

One of the vehicles came to a halt. A woman ran to it as a door slid open, disgorging a man. They both wore similar uniforms—dusky red tactical pants and tops, with yellow piping down the sleeves and arms. He could barely make out the lightning logo etched onto the chest of the uniforms. The man and woman spoke for a moment, then switched places. She climbed into the patrol vehicle, and he walked out of Barry's field of view.

Changing of the guard . . .

"Attention, citizens!" The voice came from a blaring PA system that echoed from the rooftops and redoubled in the concrete and steel canyons of the city. "Rain will commence in three . . . two . . . one . . ."

The sky, moments ago clear, black, and star-pocked, clouded over in an instant as a thick, anvil-shaped, gray-going-black cumulonimbus coalesced rapidly in the air above the city. Thunder cracked. Rain pelted him, falling in blinding sheets.

He built up his speed and darted down the side of the building. At this speed, each raindrop was a tiny, glistening bauble, hanging in the relative slowness of gravity's grasp. He batted some away and plowed through the others, carefully skipping down the exterior wall until he hit the street.

He needed to find a place to hole up, somewhere dry where he could wait out the storm and think. Given the appearance of the land just beyond the city, he wondered: What was the rest of the country like? If he ran to Star City, would it even be there? Would he be able to find Oliver Queen and the others, or at least their doppelgängers, and have them help him?

Rain sluiced down on him. Time for thinking later. Shelter was more important. He could phase into any of the buildings around him, but there were people inside. He didn't want to startle anyone, and he didn't cotton to breaking and entering in any event.

Up ahead, sandwiched in between two larger buildings, he caught sight of a smaller, three-story building that looked as though it had been left there by mistake. As though some city planner, decades ago, had started the plans for a larger building, then forgotten to finish them, and the small structure was put in place before anyone could stop it.

Better yet, there was a light coming from it. A neon sign that read OPEN. The only one he'd seen so far during his run through the city.

He dashed to it. Sure enough, the doorknob turned when he tried it, and he ducked inside, well aware that his Flash costume would probably provoke some tough questions at the very least. *One problem at a time. At least it's dry in here.*

The interior was darker than outside, even given the

cloud cover. His eyes had not yet adjusted to the murk when a familiar voice crooned, "Enter freely, and unafraid."

No. No way!

He closed the door behind him and took another step inside. A match flared to life in the darkness, and a moment later several candles burned on a table before him. And sitting at that table . . .

"Madame Xanadu!" he breathed.

Barry did not have a photographic memory, but he had a very, very good one: The interior of Madame Xanadu's shop on Earth 27 bore a striking similarity to the boardwalk cottage she'd inhabited on Earth 1. Same candles. Same mason jars and occult paraphernalia lining the shelves.

Same woman with the same ineffably knowing expression waiting for him at the table. She smiled easily at him, her eyes glowing and limpid like two liquid sapphires lit from within. A well of gratitude rose up within him, quenching a flicker of bemusement. Here, at last, was something he knew. Something if not friendly, then at least familiar.

He opened his mouth to introduce himself, but before he could speak a word, she said, "You took my advice and it worked well for you, did it not?"

Barry hesitated before sitting in the chair across from

her. "You may have me mistaken for someone else. I'm not from around here."

"You are Barry Allen." She closed her eyes for a moment, the lids quivering. When she opened them again, she said, "I read your cards. We spoke of your future." She grimaced and put her fingertips to her temples, as though massaging a headache. "We found a card that should not have existed." She frowned. "Have you divined its nature?"

Barry stood perfectly still for a moment, considering. He remembered the card—its twining borders and its black dot in the midst of white. But how could *she* remember it? Unless . . .

Was this the Madame Xanadu of Earth 1, having hopped to Earth 27, too? The odds of him stumbling upon Earth 27's Madame Xanadu were already astronomical—the odds of her independently coming to the same universe as one he'd accidentally happened upon *and* showing up in his path seemed incalculably large.

Then again, it *was* Madame Xanadu. As much as he hated to admit it, it seemed as though a lot of what he thought of as "normal" just didn't apply to her.

"Wait!" Barry slapped a palm on the table. Madame Xanadu did not flinch in the slightest. "You're not from my universe! Your eyes were *green* on Earth 1." He remembered now—they'd been as preternaturally verdant as her eyes were now azure. "How do you know who I am, then?"

"Earth 1?" She frowned. "I'm unfamiliar with this term."

"Stop it. There are multiple Earths. You have to know that."

"Well, yes. Of course. There are many, many worlds, Barry. But why would one choose to use something as prosaic as *numbers* to define them?"

Barry blinked. He'd never really considered that. Numbers were a simple way to define things, to organize and categorize them. Why use anything else?

"Your system implicitly presents a hierarchy that imputes values to each universe relative to the others. Is your *Earth 1* more important than that which you would designate *Earth 52*? Or are both unique and thus uniquely valuable and valued?"

Another thing he'd never considered. He so casually used terms like *Earth 2* or *Earth 3* with friends because he'd found those Earths after his own. Of course to him, his world would be Earth 1. But when he spoke to Jay or Harry or Jesse or Kara, did they think he was denigrating their worlds? They'd said nothing, but then again, friends often let other friends' slights go unchallenged.

"That's something for me to consider," he admitted. "But it's not why I'm here. There was an accident during my transition from one Earth to another. I need to figure out how to get home, but I also want to do what I can to help the people here. Maybe you can help me the way your doppelgänger did back home."

She shrugged and produced a deck of cards from the folds of her dress. She fanned them facedown on the table between them.

"I can tell you where to go next. But only you can choose to go there. Only you can choose which of the many paths that will radiate before you." She arched an eyebrow. "Are you ready and willing?"

Barry clenched his jaw. Oh, yes, he was ready and willing.

Soon, he ran along the streets of Central City, looking for a specific address. Madame Xanadu of Earth 27 (the numbers were just *easier*, he decided) was a lot less mysterious than her Earth 1 counterpart. She checked some cards and then rattled off an address in what was—back home—a very tony district of Central City. Here, it was run-down, the buildings' facades pitted with age, windows boarded up.

At some point, he would have to figure out how she had known so much about his experiences on Earth 1. But that was a mystery for later. Right now . . .

The cards had come up with an eagle, a fish, and then

another eagle. "Two problems, one solution," Madame Xanadu had intoned, and then sent him off.

Halfway to the address, the citywide PA system blared out, "Citizens! Rain will cease in three . . . two . . . one . . ."

Like someone turning a tap, the steady flow of precipitation halted. The angry clouds parted and dissipated, unfurling to bare the night-black sky and a waxing gibbous moon hanging overhead like an overripe cantaloupe.

It would be beautiful if he weren't stuck here. It would be beautiful if it were home.

The building in question was a corner lot. Back home, it was a steel-and-glass marvel, a shimmering silver needle against the sky. Here, it was cancerous and dented, with fissures spiderwebbing its surface. Nothing stood out about it; nothing seemed out of the ordinary or exceptional.

Water dripped from broken gutters and sluiced into the sewers. He forced himself not to think of Earthworm. Joe and the others would figure that out. He could do nothing for them right now.

He paused, looking up at the unremarkable building, and scratched his head. He could phase inside, of course, and search the entire place in a few seconds, but he wanted some kind of idea of what he was walking into.

Just then someone shouted, "Now!"

Barry thought, *It's never good when you hear* that, and

then the building seemed to topple toward him, and the street folded up at his feet, and he spun himself dizzy, blessedly blacking out before smacking hard into the sidewalk.

He woke to manacles on his wrists and a bright light shining square in his eyes. A gritty, sour taste in his mouth told him that he'd vomited at some point. Delightful. He was really putting his best foot forward on Earth 27. Robbed from, shot at, rained on, knocked out, and now add *puking up his guts* to the list.

Those manacles were threaded through two substantial U-shaped bolts on a table before him. He sat in a chair that was in no way comfortable, his legs chained to the floor. Everything rattled and clinked as he tried to sit up straighter and get the light out of his eyes, but no good. He was held fast.

The thought of vibrating to phase through the chains made his stomach lurch. Whatever had been done to him, its effects still lingered.

Two shapes lurked in the dark beyond the bright light. One of them stirred and spoke in a voice that seemed familiar to him.

"I'd wager you didn't like that zap we gave you. Tell us why you were lurking outside and maybe you won't get another."

He racked his brain, trying to place the voice, but he was

still bleary and vertiginous. "I was sent here," he said. "By Madame Xanadu. She said you could help me."

The first figure turned to the second. "You know anyone named Madame Xanadu?"

The second figure's voice was gravelly and rich, also familiar. A ten-packs-of-cigarettes-a-day voice. "I ain't fancy like that," it said. "Don't know anyone goes by *Madame*."

The first figure chuckled without mirth. "Don't rightly care who sent you," he said. "At first we thought you were him, but now that we see you up close, we're not so sure."

"Him who?" Barry asked. He was stalling for time. Once he could shake off the effects of whatever they'd done to him, he'd be a prisoner no longer.

The shadow-shrouded heads turned, clearly exchanging glances with each other. When Number One spoke again, it was in a tone that told Barry they thought he was a complete dunce. "*Him*, you idiot. Johnny Quick."

"Who's Johnny Quick?"

The first turned to the second. "Either he's got brain damage or he thinks we're stupid."

The second responded, "Why can't it be both?"

Suddenly, it clicked into place. The voices. They were familiar because . . .

"Snart?" He ducked his head, trying to get the light out of his eyes and see past it. "Rory?"

Silence for a moment. The two figures went totally still.

"How do you know those names?" Number One asked after a moment. Hearing it again, Barry was certain he was right. "Are you a Quickling? You don't dress like one, but you don't dress like one of us, either."

The second figure sighed. "He knows us. No point to the third degree."

"Fine." Number One leaned over and snapped off the light. Barry blinked spots out of his eyes, and when he refocused, yes, he was looking directly into the eyes of his old foes, the Rogues of Central City: Captain Cold and Heat Wave.

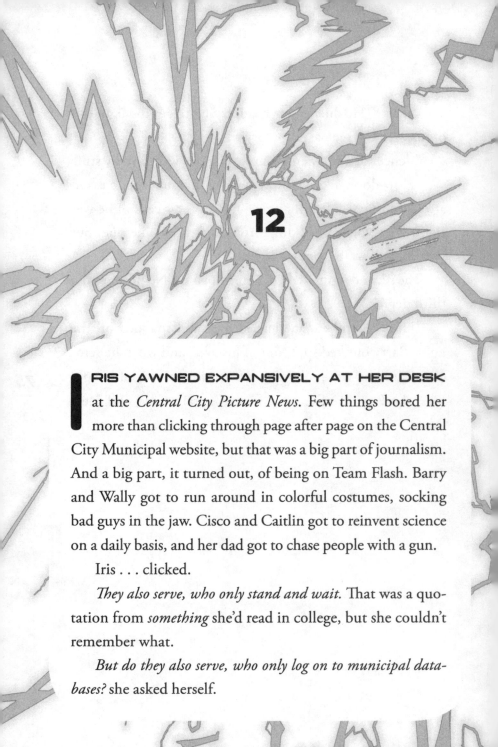

12

IRIS YAWNED EXPANSIVELY AT HER DESK at the *Central City Picture News*. Few things bored her more than clicking through page after page on the Central City Municipal website, but that was a big part of journalism. And a big part, it turned out, of being on Team Flash. Barry and Wally got to run around in colorful costumes, socking bad guys in the jaw. Cisco and Caitlin got to reinvent science on a daily basis, and her dad got to chase people with a gun.

Iris . . . clicked.

They also serve, who only stand and wait. That was a quotation from *something* she'd read in college, but she couldn't remember what.

But do they also serve, who only log on to municipal databases? she asked herself.

She was having no luck with a general records search. An old journalism professor, Professor Ryder, had once told her that "organization is the heart of research." So she went old-school and drew up a little chart: all of the people they either knew or suspected to be the Earthworm's victims so far, including names and causes of death.

Nothing significant that she could tell. But she felt a little better just having the information in front of her.

Strumming her fingers on her desk, she stared at her computer screen. Then, on an impulse, she typed "Madame Xanadu" into the search box for the *Picture News* database. If the mysterious fortune-teller had ever been mentioned in the newspaper, she would know right . . . about . . .

Now.

Nothing. *No results returned,* the database told her.

She tried a more general search, querying some of the professional databases the newspaper subscribed to: legal indexes, medical databases, that sort of thing.

More nothing.

All right, then . . . What the heck. She tried just Googling *Madame Xanadu.*

For the separate words, there were a bunch of French hits, and for "Xanadu" there was a movie and the famous poem, but for the words together, as a unit . . .

Zip. Zilch. Nada.

Well, so much for that. I guess there's nothing out there about her. Moving on . . .

She stopped that line of thinking. Something had just occurred to her.

What were the odds of there being *nothing* out there on Madame Xanadu? Nothing on the entire Internet? Really? On the *entire Internet?* How was that even possible?

Figure Madame Xanadu was a recluse. And a technophobe. Fine. She wouldn't be on any sort of social media or even have a website. That was believable.

But she had to apply for a business license, right? She had to file for a sales permit, right? She had to pay city taxes. There would be records of those things in the municipal database.

Maybe, Iris, you dolt, "Madame Xanadu" isn't her real name. Duh.

But it was the name of her business, at the very least. That should have popped up somewhere.

And am I supposed to believe that none of the people who've visited her have ever posted on social media? No one ever took a selfie outside her building and Insta'd "just had my palm read— I'm totes gonna be rich! lol #madamexanadu #forreals #blessed"?

That no one had ever done so seemed ridiculous. And improbable.

There were only two possibilities. One was that Barry had hallucinated both of his encounters with "Madame

Xanadu." That she was a figment of his imagination. That notion disturbed her. She didn't want to think Barry was losing his mind, so she didn't let herself.

And then there was the card. The card that Barry had given to her before traipsing off into the Multiverse. She scrutinized it now. The second possibility . . .

The second possibility was even crazier than the idea that Barry was losing his mind. She couldn't quite bring herself to believe that magic was—

"West!" The cry shook her out of her thoughts. Its source was Scott Evans, her editor, who stood over her. "Are you daydreaming, or are you reporting on something?"

She grinned up at him sheepishly. "Right at this moment? Neither. Right at this moment, I'm listening to my wise and insightful and understanding editor."

Evans grunted. "Flattery will get you far in life, West, but not today and not with me. I have three reporters out sick and CCPD just recovered a body. I need you to get the story." He hooked a thumb over his shoulder. "Parker's your photographer. He's got the details. Get moving."

CCPD was still on the scene when Iris and Parker arrived. She noted with a mix of resignation and regret that the crime scene tech was, of course, not Barry.

The scene was an alleyway. Because where else would

you dump a dead body? The police had both ends cordoned off with yellow crime scene tape, but that wouldn't stop her from looking in.

"Detective West!" she called out to her father, who stood behind the crime scene tape, fists planted on his hips as he stared down at the body. "Care to offer a comment for the *Picture News*?"

Joe looked over at her, delight and annoyance making an interesting collage of his expression. Dad and detective at war on his face.

Detective won. "No reporters," he told her.

His cop voice. She was used to it. Had grown up hearing it. Her father was in the running for sainthood, as far as Iris was concerned, but he was still a parent and he'd had to bring the Dad Hammer down a few times when she and Barry had been kids. There'd been the time they'd tried to rappel from the garage roof. The time they'd stuffed oatmeal in the DVD player. (Barry had a theory about lasers.) The time they'd decided to adopt every stray cat in the neighborhood . . . and a surly raccoon, too. And then there was what was still referred to only as "the Cake Batter Incident," which was the only time in her life she'd ever seen Joe West completely blow his stack. So the cop voice didn't scare her.

Parker was already snapping pictures of the body and the scene. This particular alleyway was near the Central City

Museum. "Kind of hoity-toity for a body dump, isn't it, Detective?" she asked, holding out her phone to record his response.

The other cops snickered in Joe's general direction. He stomped over to her and put a hand over her phone. "What are you doing?" he whispered.

"My job," she said with as much sweetness as she could muster. "Like you, Detective."

Joe ground his teeth together, then finally spoke in a very measured voice: "CCPD has no comment at this time. You can check for updates with the Public Information Office." He paused. "I can give you the number, if you need it."

For questioning her journalistic bona fides, she kicked him—lightly—in the shin under the crime scene tape. Joe grinned broadly. "Just doing *my* job," he said.

"We're not gonna get anything here," she told Parker. "Let's go. I'll check with the PIO in an hour and see what they have for us."

As they turned to leave, Joe called out, "Oh, hey, Ms. West!"

Iris stepped away from Parker, back to the crime scene tape. Joe leaned over and, after making sure her phone was tucked away, whispered, "Off the record, this looks like it might be another Earthworm deal."

It took a moment for Iris to make the connection. She

nodded. "He's getting upscale, then. From the recycling plant to the museum."

Joe shrugged. "You know what the real estate agents say: *Location, location, location.*"

Iris nodded along, but suddenly a thought occurred to her. "Dad! Location! That's it!"

"What's 'it'?" Joe asked irritably, but Iris was already running away from him, barking into her cell phone.

"What's 'it'?" he yelled again after her, even though he knew it was pointless.

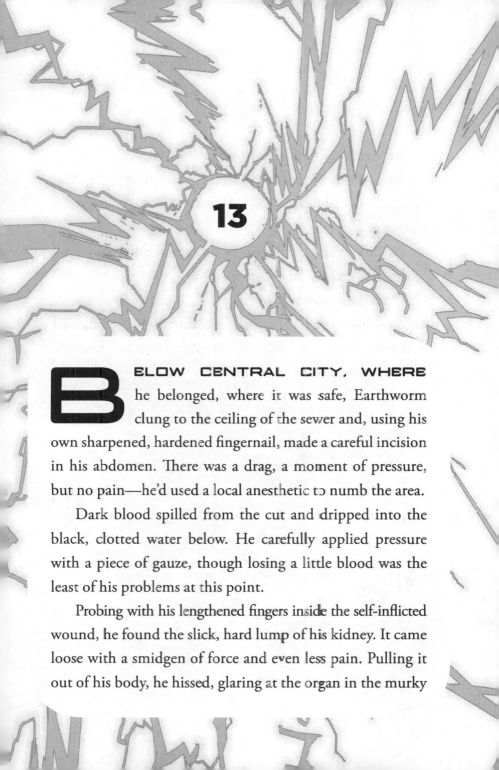

13

BELOW CENTRAL CITY, WHERE he belonged, where it was safe, Earthworm clung to the ceiling of the sewer and, using his own sharpened, hardened fingernail, made a careful incision in his abdomen. There was a drag, a moment of pressure, but no pain—he'd used a local anesthetic to numb the area.

Dark blood spilled from the cut and dripped into the black, clotted water below. He carefully applied pressure with a piece of gauze, though losing a little blood was the least of his problems at this point.

Probing with his lengthened fingers inside the self-inflicted wound, he found the slick, hard lump of his kidney. It came loose with a smidgen of force and even less pain. Pulling it out of his body, he hissed, glaring at the organ in the murky sewer light. The kidney was rotted and stony hard, useless and dead.

Releasing it, he let it drop into the water.

From a pouch, he carefully withdrew an ice-filled bag, which contained in it one of the kidneys he'd taken from the Upworlder.

He didn't think of them as victims. Not really. They were . . . libations. Oblations. *Offerings*.

Once, he'd been an Upworlder. That seemed so long ago. Another life. Another person. And then light had flashed in the sky. Rain poured down. And he changed. The world above became useless and corrosive to him; only below, in the dark and in the damp, could he be safe.

Down in the sewers. A better place. A safer place.

But even here was not perfect. Even here, he wasted away.

With sure, confident fingers, he plucked the kidney, glimmering pink with ice-diluted blood, from the bag, and slipped it into the incision. He held it in place and felt his own body extrude tendrils to enfold the new organ, absorbing it into place, mooring it to the necessary blood vessels and nerves.

He stitched the incision and clung there to the ceiling for long moments. Already, he could tell that the kidney—though fresh and healthy—would do him no good. It was a temporary fix at best.

Fortunately, there were more where that came from. Upworld.

There were organs aplenty in Upworld. Hundreds of thousands of oblations, hundreds of thousands of offerings, all for the taking . . .

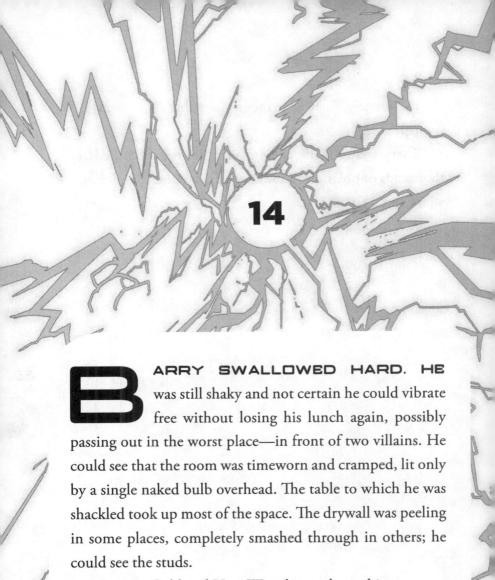

14

BARRY SWALLOWED HARD. HE was still shaky and not certain he could vibrate free without losing his lunch again, possibly passing out in the worst place—in front of two villains. He could see that the room was timeworn and cramped, lit only by a single naked bulb overhead. The table to which he was shackled took up most of the space. The drywall was peeling in some places, completely smashed through in others; he could see the studs.

Captain Cold and Heat Wave loomed over him.

"Look, whatever you guys are up to—" he started.

"Up to?" Heat Wave—Mick Rory—snorted.

"As if you didn't know," Captain Cold—Leonard Snart—insinuated, leaning forward, elbows on the table.

"Why else were you skulking around outside?"

"I told you: Madame Xanadu—"

"Who we've never heard of."

"Well, she's heard of you, because she sent me here for help."

"Help!" Heat Wave snorted and leaned back against the remains of a wall. "You come here dressed in lightning and want help from *us*?"

"You loiter around the building, a place no one's supposed to know about. Dressed almost exactly like you-know-who—"

"I *don't* know who. That's what I'm trying to tell you."

Captain Cold and Heat Wave looked at each other. Heat Wave shrugged. "He sounds earnest to me."

"I can't believe you want to trust someone wearing the lightning," Captain Cold complained.

"I didn't say *that*."

Trust. Something in that word jogged Barry's brain, kicked it back into gear. Trust. The Rogues didn't trust anybody. That was what made them Rogues. But now they were panicked and concerned about trust?

He remembered the graveyard. Everyone was dead. *Cisco* was dead. And if Cisco had died shortly after the particle accelerator explosion, then that meant . . .

"He never built a cold gun," Barry murmured. "You're

not Captain Cold." He looked from Snart to Rory. "And you're not Heat Wave."

Mick Rory blinked rapidly several times. "How hard did you hit him with the gun, Len? He's talking gibberish."

It was the opposite here on Earth 27, he realized. On Earth 27, Leonard Snart and Mick Rory were *good guys*, just as Caitlin and Cisco had been evil on Earth 2. *That's* why Madame Xanadu sent him here—she was sending him to the people who could help him.

"Guys, let's cut through the nonsense, OK?" He gritted his teeth and took a deep breath, then vibrated the molecules of his physical form until the manacles dropped through him and clanked unceremoniously to the floor. He stopped as soon as he heard that clank, his head still woozy.

"You *are* him!" Mick shouted.

"Oh God!" Len's eyes danced with terror. "We're dead!"

"Guys!" Barry stood up and held his hands out, palms up. "Guys, I'm not whoever it is you're scared of. I did that to show you can trust me. I could have done much worse, right?"

Barry had to admit that a part of him enjoyed their fear. On Earth 1, Captain Cold and Heat Wave were the meanest, snarkiest, most annoyingly dauntless of the Rogues. Nothing intimidated them. The Earth 27 varieties were quaking in their boots at the merest indication of his speed.

But he wasn't here to frighten people. Not even those who wore the faces of his enemies.

"I'm truly here for your help," he told them. "I'm not going to hurt you."

"What do you want?" Len asked, and there was a little steel in his voice, a little of the insouciance he'd come to expect from Captain Cold.

"Believe it or not, I'm looking for a magic wand. But why don't we start with you telling me who Johnny Quick is, and why you're so afraid of him?"

Len and Mick looked at each other. They shared a brief moment of silence, and then Mick sighed.

"OK. Here goes . . ."

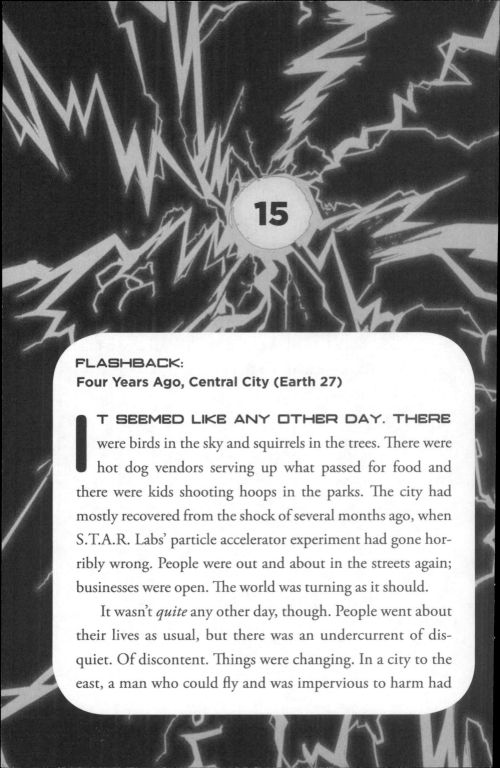

15

FLASHBACK:
Four Years Ago, Central City (Earth 27)

IT SEEMED LIKE ANY OTHER DAY. THERE were birds in the sky and squirrels in the trees. There were hot dog vendors serving up what passed for food and there were kids shooting hoops in the parks. The city had mostly recovered from the shock of several months ago, when S.T.A.R. Labs' particle accelerator experiment had gone horribly wrong. People were out and about in the streets again; businesses were open. The world was turning as it should.

It wasn't *quite* any other day, though. People went about their lives as usual, but there was an undercurrent of disquiet. Of discontent. Things were changing. In a city to the east, a man who could fly and was impervious to harm had declared himself a king. In Coast City, there were reports of—it sounded silly just to say it—a man with a glowing, magic ring who had taken over.

But surely nothing like that would happen here. Not in Central City.

That night, however, it started.

He broke in on all the local television channels. Word spread quickly; TVs were turned on, channels switched. And pretty much the entire population of Central City saw him for the first time in that moment.

A red cowl covered his hair and ears and the sides of his face, but left everything from eyebrows to chin exposed. Not that the exposure mattered—his face was blurred somehow. Most people thought it was a special effect, some sort of camera filter. Soon enough, they would learn that it was his superspeed in action.

Flaring out from the ears of the cowl: two long, jagged, yellow lightning bolts, curving up along his head.

When he spoke, his voice was a tremolo, wavering and varied, impossible to identify.

He was brief and to the point:

"There are eight hundred thousand people living in Central City," he said. "I am going to kill ten percent of them."

And thirty seconds later, he'd done just that.

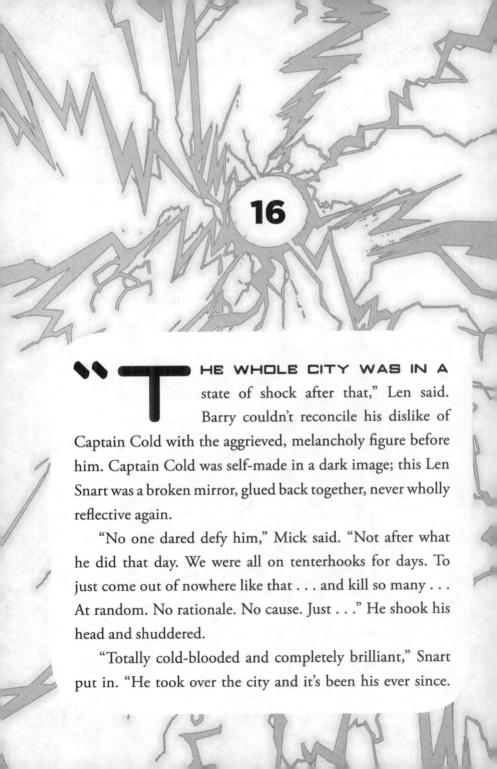

16

"**T**HE WHOLE CITY WAS IN A state of shock after that," Len said. Barry couldn't reconcile his dislike of Captain Cold with the aggrieved, melancholy figure before him. Captain Cold was self-made in a dark image; this Len Snart was a broken mirror, glued back together, never wholly reflective again.

"No one dared defy him," Mick said. "Not after what he did that day. We were all on tenterhooks for days. To just come out of nowhere like that . . . and kill so many . . . At random. No rationale. No cause. Just . . ." He shook his head and shuddered.

"Totally cold-blooded and completely brilliant," Snart put in. "He took over the city and it's been his ever since.

Once he showed how powerful he was, you had people lining up to be on the winning side. *His* side. Next thing you know, the city is sealed off and he's got an army of Quicklings at his disposal."

"Claimed it was all for our own good," Len said in an incredulous tone. "To protect us from the others."

"What about the army?" Barry asked. "What about the government?"

Mick shook his head. "Have you been living in a cave for the past four years? Do you really not know about the Syndicate?"

Barry sighed. He didn't have time for a complete historical rundown of Earth 27. And was there any way to explain about the Multiverse that wouldn't involve more questions than answers? He didn't think so.

Johnny Quick, though—*that* was something he could deal with. Another speedster. He'd defeated Reverse-Flash and Zoom; he figured he could help this version of Central City by taking down its tyrant.

"Let's stay local for now," he told them. "Tell me a little more about Johnny Quick."

Len shrugged. "He moves like you. That's why we thought . . . Well, that and the costume. You kinda looked like a Quickling."

"Quickling. Those are the people wearing the lightning insignia? The ones I saw outside the wall?"

"You looked outside the wall?" Mick seemed impressed.

"Yeah. What happened outside the city?" He thought back to the apocalyptic landscape he'd espied from the rooftop.

Snart shrugged. "Quick happened."

"He has some way of controlling the weather," Rory growled. "Early on, he did all kinds of crazy stuff. Tornadoes, derechos, lightning storms, monsoons. Made no sense."

"We think he was calibrating the equipment he uses," Len offered. "The local ecology took a real beating. Bonus for Quick, though—it makes exile a lot bigger threat. Most people fall in line just to avoid having to go out and survive in that."

"And you guys are . . . what? The Rebel Alliance?"

Mick actually blushed. "We actually call ourselves Rogues."

The corner of Barry's mouth twitched up into a half smile. He didn't think that word could inspire joy in him, but somehow it did. A reminder of home. Plus, he was starting to feel a flutter of pity for Snart and Rory—calling themselves the Rogues made them seem not quite as pathetic.

"How did you knock me out?" he asked. His head was no longer spinning and he figured he could keep his lunch down now. But he wanted to know what to be on the lookout for.

"Oh. This." From the folds of his trench coat, Mick produced a small gadget the size and shape of a soup bowl. Made of polished aluminum, it had a black handle grafted onto it. The open end was covered in a sparkling green glass. "It's a . . . What's it called again?" he asked, turning to Len.

"Audio wavelength neural something or other," Snart said with a shrug. "Our tech genius has been working on this for a while. We plan to use it on the Quicklings, but it's really designed to take down Quick himself. Causes a massive inner-ear imbalance."

"Doesn't matter how fast you move if you don't know which way is up," Mick rumbled.

"Tech genius?"

"Guy named Hartley," Len said. "Come on. We'll show you around."

Hartley . . . Hartley Rathaway, no doubt. On Earth 1, he was the Pied Piper. First a supervillain and then a hero. It was good to know that on Earth 27 Hartley was still alive, and that he was on the side of the angels.

They allowed him out of the room and into a long corridor with regularly spaced doors.

"This place was supposed to be a hotel," Snart said. "Opening day was scheduled for six weeks after Quick's impromptu TV performance. Needless to say, it never opened. Sat abandoned for a couple of years before the boss decided to move us in. Now it's Rogues HQ."

"The boss?"

Rory gave Snart a significant look. Len nodded imperceptibly and Rory set off down the hall on his own.

"Maybe later," Snart said.

He took Barry down the hall and then down a flight of stairs, ill-lit and chilly. Moss grew on one wall. The structure had never been brought into compliance with the building code, and now probably never would be. Barry's Flash suit was superthin to provide as little wind resistance as possible. He shivered. The shiver gave him an idea and he vibrated ever so slightly, just enough to provide a little friction warmth.

Snart stared at him. "You won't make any friends around here doing that."

"Sorry." Barry stopped.

"For that matter, you won't make any friends dressed like that, either." He shook out of his coat and offered it to Barry, who slipped into it. After a moment's hesitation, he pulled down his cowl. He felt vulnerable with his face exposed, but Snart gave no indication that he recognized Barry Allen, no matter which Earth he hailed from.

One floor down, they emerged onto a mezzanine overlooking what was intended to be a hotel lobby. Instead, it was crudely divided into sections with ad hoc walls made of plywood, almost like a series of office cubicles. People scurried about, perhaps two dozen of them, moving efficiently and quietly. There was a palpable urgency that hung in the air like humidity.

"What are they doing?" Barry asked.

"Surviving," Len told him. "Trying to make progress. We have people throughout the city. They bring us data, whatever they can find. Patrol patterns. Security system upgrades. Even the rare Johnny Quick sighting. We gather it here, collate it, look for weak spots."

It was the same work ethic Captain Cold applied to his thieving, Barry knew, now broadened and applied to a beneficent purpose.

"Rare sighting?"

Len chuckled and leaned on the mezzanine railing, looking down at the cluster below. "When you have the Quicklings and the wasteland beyond the city you don't need to put in a great deal of personal appearances. Plus, half the time when he *does* come out of that sealed-off bunker of his, he moves too fast for anyone to see anything useful."

Sealed-off bunker. The old S.T.A.R. Labs complex. Johnny Quick had bricked himself up in there and was running the city from the safety of a facility designed to withstand the unleashing of the very forces of nature itself. Smart move. S.T.A.R. Labs' concentric ring design meant that any assassination attempt would have to penetrate multiple layers of security to get to their target. And even then, Johnny Quick would have the advantage of being able to control the entire complex from the safety of the Cortex. For someone really dedicated to locking the place down, S.T.A.R. Labs would make a heck of an impenetrable fortress.

"Speaking of which . . ." Len snapped Barry out of his reverie when he pointed to a man down on the lobby level. "Ralph!" he called.

The man looked around, looked up, then pointed to himself with a *Who, me?* look. Then he jogged up a flight of stairs and ambled over to them. He was tall and rangy, with a mop of red hair, a curiously twitchy nose, and an intense, intimidating mien. As he approached, he took an aggressive swig from a can of soda.

"Ralph Dibny," Len said by way of introduction. "Ralph handles smuggling operations for us, as well as overseeing our spying efforts. He's also the man who's spent days of his life staring at the video footage of Johnny Quick to try to assemble some kind of profile."

They shook hands. "Pretty diverse set of interests," Barry said.

"I like to stretch myself," Ralph said with a sneer.

"A profile of Johnny Quick?" Barry asked. "Are you a cop?"

Dibny grunted something barely audible. "No. But I think Quick is. Or was."

A chill tiptoed up Barry's spine and set up camp at the base of his neck. "Why do you say that?"

With an exaggerated eye roll, Dibny said, "Certain vocabulary tics, OK? He uses the word *perpetrate* a lot, other terms usually associated with police jargon. There's a whole range of things." He glanced at Len. "Can I *go* now?"

"You a psychologist?" Barry asked.

Clearly at the limits of his patience, Dibny frowned. "Special Forces, Psychological Warfare, back in the day. Just got a nose for this kind of thing, is all." Ralph narrowed his eyes as he looked Barry up and down. "You really got speed?"

Barry remembered Mick Rory separating from them and running on ahead. He must have given Dibny a heads-up. "Yeah."

Ralph nodded soberly. "Hope it's enough." He raised his soda can in salute and returned to the lower floor.

"He's pretty intense," Barry said once he was alone again with Len.

Len shrugged. "Yeah, he's a pretty scary dude. But he's *our* scary dude.

"And this," he continued, sweeping his arm out to encompass the entirety of the lobby floor, "is our humble abode. The heartbeat of the Rogues, where we plan to throw our bodies against Johnny Quick's battlements. We don't have much, but maybe, just maybe, we can help you." He fixed Barry with a stare that was almost—*almost*—as intense as that of his Earth 1 counterpart. "If you help us first."

"How?" As if he couldn't guess.

"You move like him," Len said. "You even sound like him, but it's tough to tell with that thing he does where he vibrates his voice. Maybe you're the key to defeating him. You help out and maybe we can get your magic wand back."

Barry drew in a deep breath and weighed his words carefully. There were two ways to respond: the savvy way and the honest way.

He couldn't help himself; he went with honest.

"I'll help you whether you can get the wand back or not," he said. "If you can get it for me, that's great, and I'd be obliged. But I won't stand by and let people suffer like this. Not when I have the power to help."

Len nodded and grinned in a very non–Captain Cold–like manner. "I think it's time for you to meet the boss."

A tight, dark corridor behind what would have been the hotel's front desk led to a plain wooden door with a simple knob. Mick Rory stood outside the door, his hands clasped before him, looking for all the world like an almost lifelike statue.

At a nod from Len, Mick came to life, opening the door.

"Meet the boss," Mick said, gesturing for Barry to enter.

Barry stepped inside, mind racing, speculating on which Earth 27 version would be in charge of the resistance to Johnny Quick. Would it be Captain Singh? Maybe his old girlfriend, Patty Spivot. Or Kendra Saunders or maybe even Ollie Queen . . .

None of them. He froze in shock at what he saw.

The room was small, cramped, with an old chair sitting before a scarred steel desk clearly scavenged from an office that had long been decommissioned. The walls were dark paneled, chipped and patched here and there.

Behind the desk, blinds were pulled down to cover the wall. And sitting at the desk . . .

"Trickster!" Barry breathed.

James Jesse pursed his lips and shook his head. "No time for tricks, son. This is deadly serious business."

On Earth 1, James Jesse had been the criminal known as the Trickster, a sociopath who used the tools and gimmicks of a prankster to terrorize Central City for years. Locked up for life in Iron Heights before Barry had become the Flash, he'd escaped recently, manipulating his estranged son in an attempt to wreak vengeance on the city and its people.

On Earth 27, he was . . .

"You're in charge?" Barry asked. "*You're* the leader of the Rogues?"

Jesse cleared his throat and stroked his beard. "Have we crossed paths before? Have I wronged you somehow?"

Not entirely. But a man who looked and sounded *exactly* the same had set off bombs all over Central City and had taken Barry's father hostage. It wasn't easy to shake that off and pretend that this man was the hope of the city.

"I know someone who looks a lot like you," Barry said. "Just sort of threw me."

Jesse nodded gravely. "Tough times. We all get thrown for a loop on a daily basis, it seems. Ever since that Crimson Comet crashed headlong into my town and made it over in his image. You from around here?"

Barry chose his words carefully. "I'm familiar with the area."

Jesse leaned back in his chair and rubbed his eyes. "So. Johnny Quick . . . Here's what we know: Fast. Obviously. Crazy fast. They told you about his initial killing spree?"

"Yes."

"Well, he's only gotten faster since then. We think he stumbled upon something. Something that amped up his speed."

Barry considered that. He'd increased his own speed through tortuous, repetitious practice, but there *were* shortcuts. Maybe Quick had developed his own version of Velocity-9, the speed-enhancing drug that Zoom had manipulated Caitlin into creating.

"The army was supposed to come in," James Jesse continued. "The FBI . . . But they got caught up in other cities, with the other ones. And pretty soon, after some superpowered warfare, there wasn't much left to take him on."

"What other ones?"

"Have you been living under a rock, son?" Jesse asked with surprising gentleness. Or maybe it wasn't surprising on Earth 27. On Earth 1, if James Jesse had evinced the slightest micron of empathy, Barry would have assumed it was a ruse, panicked, and started looking for the exits.

"I've been . . . out of touch."

Jesse grunted a syllable that seemed to say, *I'll accept that . . . for now.* He stood and raised the blinds behind him. Instead of a window, there was a map of the United States there, but one Barry had never seen before. Chunks of Canada were included in New York State and North Dakota. California was large pieces around San Diego and the Bay Area. A big slice of Mexico was labeled "South Texas."

There were other differences, but what jumped out at him were five icons positioned near cities. Over Central City was the dual lightning stroke image he'd become accustomed to. But there was a sort of stylized green infinity symbol adjacent to Coast City. And then three icons along the Eastern Seaboard—an owl's head, an S in a circle, and a U in an inverted triangle.

"The Crime Syndicate of America," Jesse said, tapping the map at each of the five icons. "When the particle accelerator blew, it empowered five of the world's evilest, most vile and sadistic criminals, giving them superpowers beyond anything any of us have ever seen."

"Just those five?" Barry asked. It didn't seem to make sense. On every other Earth he'd encountered, the explosion had indiscriminately made metas of dozens of people, some good, some evil, some in between.

"As far as anyone knows, yeah, just these five." Jesse sighed and rubbed his hands together, gazing at the map. "One of them set an entire mountain range on fire, just to cordon off part of the East Coast. Quick claims he's acting in our best interests, protecting us from the others."

"That's usually how tyrants roll," Barry said. "They tell you things would be so much worse without them."

Jesse nodded. "Every now and then there's a rumor that maybe someone good—or even just *normal*—got the powers, too, but it never pans out." He raised an eyebrow significantly at Barry. "Until now."

Barry became aware of Len and Mick standing just behind him. He imagined Mick had that neurological weapon locked and loaded, just in case this whole thing was a ruse after all.

"I'm here to help," Barry said.

"I'm glad to hear that," Jesse said. "You might be just the break we need. We've spent years studying Quick's troops and their systems, their patterns, but we only ever see him for snatches of seconds at a time. He runs the city. He runs *everything*. He controls the *weather*, for God's sake!"

Jesse's face had gone red with outrage. He steadied himself on the desk and took a deep breath. Visibly relaxed, he sank into his chair.

"We need intel on *him*," he went on. "And as far as we can tell, the only time he's ever relaxed down to normal speed is when he's inside that fortress of his. Can you do that thing he does where he runs through walls?"

Len spoke up. "Yeah, he can."

Barry saw where this was headed. "I can. But I won't know the lay of the land in there. It's risky. Is there someone on the outside who might know what it looks like inside?"

The three Rogues shared a knowing chuckle. James Jesse grinned. "Why, yes."

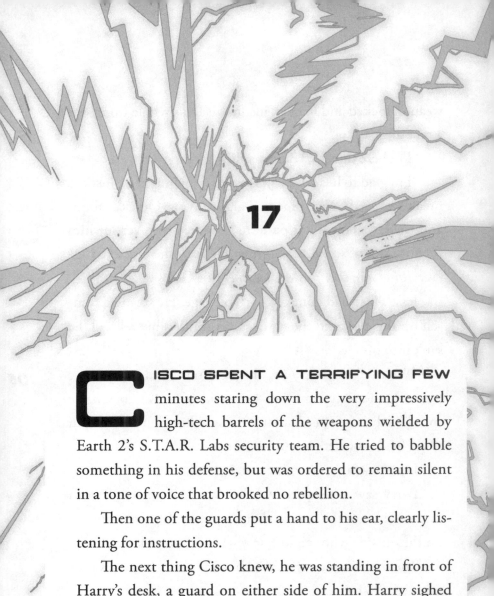

17

CISCO SPENT A TERRIFYING FEW minutes staring down the very impressively high-tech barrels of the weapons wielded by Earth 2's S.T.A.R. Labs security team. He tried to babble something in his defense, but was ordered to remain silent in a tone of voice that brooked no rebellion.

Then one of the guards put a hand to his ear, clearly listening for instructions.

The next thing Cisco knew, he was standing in front of Harry's desk, a guard on either side of him. Harry sighed wearily and dismissed the guards with a flick of his fingers.

"Ramon," Harry rasped, his voice freighted with exasperation. "What were you thinking?"

"I was thinking I'd bop over the interdimensional barrier

and see my old buddy Harry, but apparently you greet compadres with guns over here on Earth 2. WTHeck, Harry?"

Wells groaned theatrically and did that Clint Eastwood squint that he'd perfected, the one Cisco had practiced in the mirror a million times and never once gotten right. "No, we only call out the guns when super villains march into the building and announce themselves. Your doppelgänger here is dead, but *Cisco Ramon a.k.a. Vibe* is still listed in the security databases as a threat."

Cisco harrumphed with righteous indignation and straightened his shirt. "Maybe you guys should update your databases, then. It's been months since Evil Cisco took the dirt nap from which there is no waking."

"Super-people have an annoying tendency to come back from the dead," Harry growled. "Now, what can I do for you, Ramon?"

Cisco told him about Hocus Pocus, the wand, and Barry's decision to come to Earth 2 for help. "Without waiting for me to open a breach, might I add!" he complained. That had been hours ago and everyone back on Earth 1 was getting antsy.

As Cisco told his story, Harry leaned back in his chair and steepled his fingers before him. Cisco started to feel the pit of his stomach contracting into a tight, nauseated ball. Harry clearly had no idea what Cisco was talking about.

"None of this is ringing a bell, eh?" he asked.

Harry simply shook his head.

"You haven't seen Barry, have you?"

"Haven't seen Allen for months," Harry told him. "Not since Jesse and I left Earth 1 to come home."

"Aw, crap." Cisco blew out a long, shuddering breath. Great. Barry had never made it to Earth 2. Now he had to go home and tell Team Flash that for now they were just . . . Team.

"Good seeing you, Harry," he said, heading for the door. "Always nice to catch up. Ask your guards not to shoot me on my way out, OK?"

Iris called the Public Information Office at CCPD, got some details on the case, and filed a quick story for the *Picture News* website. She promised Scott she'd stay on the story and file an update when more information was available.

Then she drove out to S.T.A.R. Labs. She hoped that maybe Barry would be back from Earth 2 by now, but as soon as she entered the Cortex, she saw that it was only Caitlin and H.R., listless and moping.

"Guys, I think I have a lead on this Earthworm character."

Caitlin perked up and H.R. cracked a grin. "Some good news. At last!" H.R. rat-a-tatted on the edge of a desk with his drumsticks.

"What did you learn?" Caitlin asked.

"Well, I was thinking about locations, and it occurred to me that . . ."

She trailed off as Cisco strode into the Cortex. He seemed shaken to see her there, as though he'd hoped not to have to see her.

Which meant . . .

Bad news. Barry wasn't with him. So . . .

"I have good news!" Cisco crowed.

Iris's heart skipped a beat.

"Remember those Alpine White candy bars that they stopped making?" he asked.

Everyone exchanged glances. "Yeah . . ." Caitlin said slowly.

"They were pretty awesome," Iris admitted.

"They still make them on Earth 2!" Cisco dug into his pockets, produced a half-dozen white chocolate bars with almonds, and handed them out. Once everyone had peeled back the wrappers, he dropped the bad news. "Oh, and also Barry's not on Earth 2 and I don't know where he is and there's really no way to find out and please don't kill me because after all it's not my fault I was asleep."

It took a moment for everyone to absorb it. Iris swallowed hard and lowered her candy bar. Tears welled in her eyes. The room went dead silent, except for the sound of

H.R. chomping through his candy bar. After a moment, he looked up to see everyone staring at Cisco.

"Did I miss something again?" he asked. "This is just so darn good that I was really focused on the—"

"Barry's lost," Iris said, her voice cracking on the word *lost*. "Somewhere in the Multiverse."

"And let's not forget that this is *not* my fault," Cisco reminded them.

Iris threw down her candy bar and stalked over to Cisco, who stood frozen, rooted to the spot. With a stiff finger, she poked Cisco in the chest. "*You* built the harness doohickey he used to go running off into the quantum foam!"

Cisco took a step back, shaking just a little. "First of all, I'm *really* impressed at the quantum foam reference. Bravo. Second of all, if I'd been awake, I would have *told* him not to use the harness. And third of all," he said, his voice becoming strong and more powerful, "seriously, Iris, for the love of God, don't kill me, OK?"

Iris turned away from him and folded her arms over her chest, hugging herself. All her anger bled away, replaced by cold fear. "So he's out there alone?" Iris asked. "And we don't know where?"

"Can't you just vibe him?" Caitlin asked.

H.R. snapped his fingers and spoke with a mouth full of white chocolate, which crumbled and sprayed as he spoke.

"Yes! Use your vibe powers to home in on him and we'll yank him back here. I'm glad I was here to think of that."

Caitlin shot him a dirty look.

"Guys . . ." Cisco shook his head. "It doesn't work like that. First of all, the only time I've been able to pick up a vibe across dimensions was when we thought Earth 2 was going to be destroyed by Zoom. That was a big enough event to cross the barrier between universes. But let's assume I *do* vibe Barry. All I'll see is where he is. It's not like there'll be a big sign saying, 'This is Earth 247!' I'll just see whatever's around him. He might just be in a random room somewhere. It won't tell me which universe out of the fifty-two we know of to try. And even if it did, it won't tell me *where* in that universe to look." Cisco paused. "Wow, I'm being a serious bummer!"

"Yeah, maybe you don't talk for a while," Caitlin said, waving Cisco into silence and gesturing for everyone's attention. "Look, I know this is scary, but we have to remember: He's the Flash. I'm sure he'll be fine. There's nothing he can't handle. And if things get really bad, there's nothing he can't outrun."

"Or outthink," Iris said defiantly.

Cisco nodded.

"He's coming back." Iris stepped into the center of the room. All eyes were on her. "There's no negotiating, no equivocating. He's coming back. We need to proceed on that assumption."

"So what do we do now?" Caitlin asked.

"We go after Earthworm," Iris said. "Make it one less thing Barry has to worry about when he comes home."

She looked around the room. Caitlin bobbed her head and H.R. grinned. Cisco merely nodded, distracted, lost in his own thoughts. Iris realized that she couldn't stay angry at him. Cisco was doing his best. Cisco *always* did his best, and the truth was that Cisco's *best* was better than most people's. And he did that all with the enormous burden of his own intelligence.

Iris considered herself a pretty bright, capable person, but she knew that—his goofy, nerdy antics aside—Cisco was one of the top intellects on the planet. She couldn't imagine what it would be like to have that kind of weight in your brain, to have those big, crazy thoughts all competing for space and time. How could you focus on anything at all?

"Cisco?" she said. "I sort of need your help on this."

Cisco sighed heavily, still lost in his own world, then swept his hair back off his forehead. "I'm sorry," he said. "I should have—"

"You're doing everything you can," she told him, offering a smile. "And I'm going to ask for even more."

He returned the smile. "You got it. How can I help?"

She told him what she needed, and his eyebrows knitted together in something like amusement. "That's a first, I think," he told her.

"Can you do it?" she asked.

Cisco barked a laugh into the air and cracked his knuckles. "Are you kidding me? In a heartbeat."

"The Cisco Kid rides again!" H.R. yelled. When everyone gave him a withering glare, he stumbled back a step. "Do you . . . do you not have the Cisco Kid on this Earth? Say it ain't so!"

"We have one," Caitlin said. "We just don't enjoy puns as much as you do."

H.R. harrumphed and went off in search of more coffee as Cisco's fingers played the keys of his computer with the same beauty and talent as his brother's on a piano.

A little while later, Iris received an encrypted text from her father. Cisco had given them all an unbreakable, secret text channel so that they could discuss Team Flash issues without worrying about hacking.

Sorry about playing bad cop, the text read. *Off the record, you should know that this is definitely another Earthworm death. Also, see attached.*

Iris opened the attached file and caught her breath. She took a seat next to Cisco. "How are we doing?"

"Almost there," he told her, not even glancing in her direction, his gaze fixated on the screen.

"I have some more information for you."

"Shoot it to the server. I'll grab it from there."

Iris tapped at her phone. Her heart raced. Things were picking up. Things were accelerating.

Speaking of accelerating . . .

Barry, why haven't you come back yet? Where are you?

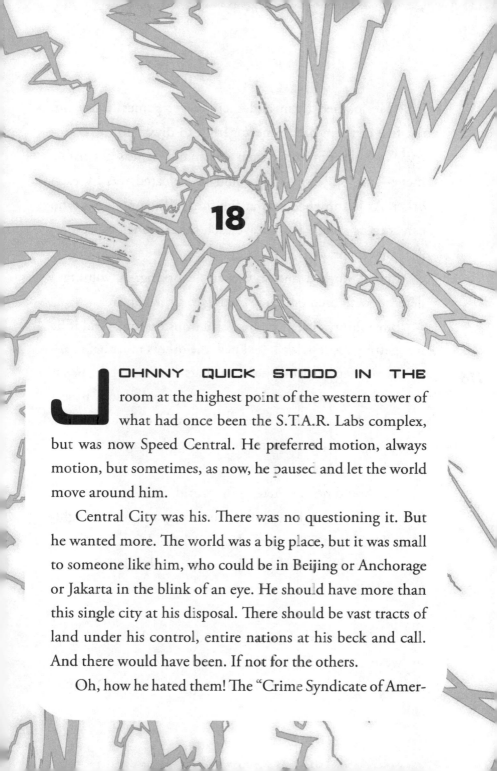

18

JOHNNY QUICK STOOD IN THE
room at the highest point of the western tower of
what had once been the S.T.A.R. Labs complex,
but was now Speed Central. He preferred motion, always
motion, but sometimes, as now, he paused and let the world
move around him.

Central City was his. There was no questioning it. But
he wanted more. The world was a big place, but it was small
to someone like him, who could be in Beijing or Anchorage
or Jakarta in the blink of an eye. He should have more than
this single city at his disposal. There should be vast tracts of
land under his control, entire nations at his beck and call.
And there would have been. If not for the others.

Oh, how he hated them! The "Crime Syndicate of America." He loathed them and their power games. Early on, the five of them had come together to divvy up the country. With the powers at their command, it was a sensible move—the only way they could be defeated was by each other. As Johnny had said at the time: "The only ones who can stop us are us. If we leave each other alone, the statues don't have a prayer."

It had worked and it was still working. A voluntary détente, with each of them sticking to a specific area.

But Johnny chafed at the restrictions on him. And if he was getting restless, well, he knew the others must be, too.

Being hemmed in by the borders of Central City was driving him mad. He could circumnavigate the globe in seconds, but he had to stay here, in this pitiful excuse for a city. Here, where chance had made him a god, pragmatism had made him a prisoner.

He should be out there in the world. Racing the oceans. Running the lengths of mountain ranges. Chasing lightning. Instead, he was cooped up in the old S.T.A.R. Labs, a protective bunker within the protective bunker that was Central City. Redundant shielding. All because he couldn't trust the others.

He was so tired of dealing with them . . . Ultraman, who he wasn't even certain was human. Superwoman, whose sheer rage and aggression actually frightened him. Owlman, whose prowess was outstripped only by his ego. And, of course, the one he hated the most, that jumped-up thug in Coast City: Power Ring.

They existed in a taut, fraught balance of mutually assured destruction. A situation that had grown untenable long ago. Perhaps the others were willing to wait and to think of the dynamics, the possible scenarios, but Quick lived in the spaces between microseconds. Every day under the current status quo grated like a century wasted and dead.

He had a sense that the first-mover advantage granted to him by his speed meant that he could take down Power Ring and Owlman and one of the other two. But at that point, his luck would run out. Superwoman or Ultraman, whoever was left, would make Johnny Quick into the World's Fastest Stain. He needed another step up. Another advantage.

Peering out over the city he ruled, he tried to will into existence a blast of scarlet and yellow on the streets below. If his soldiers were to be believed, there was another speedster out there.

Another speedster.

Johnny Quick smirked. Against *two* men who could move at the speed of light, the rest of the Crime Syndicate wouldn't stand a chance.

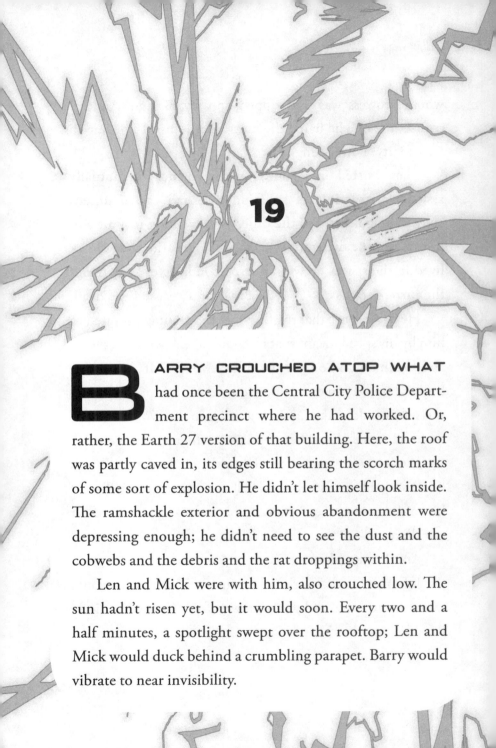

19

BARRY CROUCHED ATOP WHAT had once been the Central City Police Department precinct where he had worked. Or, rather, the Earth 27 version of that building. Here, the roof was partly caved in, its edges still bearing the scorch marks of some sort of explosion. He didn't let himself look inside. The ramshackle exterior and obvious abandonment were depressing enough; he didn't need to see the dust and the cobwebs and the debris and the rat droppings within.

Len and Mick were with him, also crouched low. The sun hadn't risen yet, but it would soon. Every two and a half minutes, a spotlight swept over the rooftop; Len and Mick would duck behind a crumbling parapet. Barry would vibrate to near invisibility.

"Shift change is right before dawn," Len told him.

Barry nodded and lifted to his eyes the binoculars the Rogues had loaned him. Down in the street, a cluster of Quicklings milled about near the First Bank of Central City. For a moment, Barry thought they might be planning on robbing it, but then reminded himself: Johnny Quick already owned the city and everything in it. He didn't need to break into a bank. He didn't even need money.

"They gather here after their patrol shift," Mick told him, "and hand off to the next shift. Then they split up and go their separate ways."

"You have to grab him after he's clocked out and separated from the others," Len warned. "If a Quickling realizes another Quickling has gone missing, it's not pretty."

"Sounds like you're speaking from experience."

Mick grunted. Len sighed. "See that?" He pointed into the distance. Barry couldn't tell what he was supposed to be seeing, and then realized that was the point. He wasn't seeing something; he was seeing the *absence* of something. Where the old Augustyn Tower had stood, there was instead a blank spot on the skyline, like a missing tooth in a grim smile.

"We tried kidnapping a Quickling once before. About a year ago. We took him to Augustyn Tower to keep our headquarters safe. Johnny Quick tore the city apart looking for his missing man. Found him—and our interrogators—in the Tower." Len bit his lip at the memory.

"What happened?" Barry asked.

Len couldn't continue, so Mick picked up the story. "He did something with his feet. Vibrations or something. It was like an earthquake—a massive one—localized right there. The whole building just came down, just crumbled into dust right in front of us." He jerked his head in Len's direction. "Len's sister was one of the interrogators. She didn't make it out. No one did."

"Lisa's dead?" Barry blurted out without thinking.

Len spun around. "How do you know my sister's name? Who *are* you?"

Barry stalled for a moment, searching for an explanation, but just then, Mick grabbed him by the shoulder. "There. Now."

Without a pause, Barry sprang into action. He ran down the side of the CCPD building, dodging divots and pulverized spots in the wall like potholes on the street. The Quickling in question had just split off from the others, heading down an alleyway, taking a shortcut to an apartment complex on the west side. The Rogues had identified this particular Quickling as a target eight months ago. He was what they called *a rotator*, an underling who rotated in and out of the S.T.A.R. Labs complex, sometimes serving inside for several weeks, at other times leading a team of lesser Quicklings out on the streets. After this particular shift, he was off duty for two days, which meant that they had forty-eight hours to get information out of him and take the fight to Johnny Quick before the King of Central City realized one of his soldiers was missing. And harrowed the city in retaliation.

Barry came up behind the Quickling at an angle and shoulder-checked the guy at Mach 3. Under normal circumstances, that would mean a bare minimum of thirty broken bones for the poor sucker, but Barry was vibrating at just the right frequency: His momentum sent the Quickling careening off at an angle, phasing through a nearby wall. Barry followed, hopping through the brick and mortar to emerge into a dingy, ill-lit room. The Quickling staggered and stumbled, collapsing right into the waiting arms of Ralph Dibny and a cluster of Rogues.

Someone produced a needle and jabbed the man in the neck, and he slumped to the floor without so much as a peep of protest.

Barry grinned. "All good?"

Ralph nodded soberly. "Yep." He knelt down and pulled off the Quickling's helmet.

It was Fred Chyre. Joe's old partner.

Barry bit his lower lip and resisted the urge to blurt something out. There was no point to exposing his shock at every reversal on Earth 27. Chyre had been a good cop on Earth 1, so it was no surprise to see him as Johnny Quick's henchman here. What *was* a surprise was seeing him alive—Fred Chyre had been killed by Clyde Mardon, the first Weather Wizard.

"Now we haul him to our interrogation site and see what we can get from him," Ralph said.

"I'll lend a hand," Barry offered.

Chyre resisted Ralph's efforts admirably. Whether it was fear or loyalty, Barry couldn't tell, but the man was adamant about not giving anything up about Johnny Quick or the layout of S.T.A.R. Labs.

The interrogation took place, Barry noted with sad irony, in the burnt-out husk of what had once been C.C. Jitters. The place looked as though a bomb had gone off there. Maybe one had. Ralph had Chyre shackled to a chair in the basement. Barry lurked in the shadows, growing impatient.

He hadn't watched very many interrogations at CCPD, but he'd grown up in a house with a very talented detective. And Joe had no problem talking about his day at the office over dinner. One tactic that often worked, Joe had said on many occasions, was to lead the person being questioned into thinking that you knew more than you actually did. If you sounded knowledgeable already, it tended to weaken their natural defenses. They stopped feeling as though they had to protect the information and entered into something more akin to a conversation with an equal.

Barry stepped out of the shadows and put a hand on Ralph's shoulder. "Let me try?"

Dibny shrugged and stepped aside. Barry dragged over a chair and sat down across from Chyre.

"Fred. Do you mind if I call you Fred?"

Chyre sneered. "You can call me vapor, kiddo. Because that's all you'll get from me."

Barry nodded as if considering that. "I think my colleague here"—he gestured to Ralph—"may have given you the wrong impression. See, we're not looking for new information. We just want you to confirm what we already know."

"You don't know anything, you greasy little punk. Johnny Quick's gonna leave footprints in your blood when he runs over you."

It was a disturbingly evocative image to process. "We know plenty. For example, at ST—at Johnny's headquarters, there are sixteen sublevels. With a mile-long circular loop underground."

Chyre's eyes narrowed in suspicion, but he said nothing.

"When you get off the elevator on the third floor," Barry said, "there's a little alcove with a water fountain and a window that looks out over the river."

Chyre's expression changed to one of shock, then quickly returned to annoyance. "Doesn't prove anything."

"Sure it does. It proves I've been inside your master's fortress. Like, for example, the medical bay just off the Cortex."

Chyre fumed. "How do you know that?"

"Like I said, Fred, we know everything. We're just confirming some details, is all. Your master is going down. You just have to decide which side you're on."

To his credit, Chyre didn't struggle very long. He blew out a long-held breath. "Fine. What do you want to know?"

"I was one of the first to sign up with him," Chyre admitted. "Right after the Big Kill."

"When he wiped out ten percent of the city."

"Yeah. Didn't make sense to resist, you know?" He flicked his gaze around the room—Len, Mick, and James had joined Barry and Ralph by now. "Anyway, a bunch of us cops signed up right away."

Barry shared a significant look with Ralph. If things were generally opposite on Earth 27, then probably most of the CCPD had been corrupt anyway. So, yeah, it made sense for a bunch of dirty cops to cozy up to a superpowered crook like Johnny Quick.

"First thing he had us do was fortify the old S.T.A.R. Labs complex. 'I want it impenetrable,' he said."

"Why? With his powers—"

"Even Johnny Quick's gotta sleep, right?" Len said.

Chyre nodded. "Plus, he had stuff in there he didn't want anyone getting their hands on."

"Like the tech he uses to control the weather?" Ralph asked.

Chyre shrugged. "I guess. I try not to ask questions. Sometimes the answers ain't worth it, you know?"

"How did he get faster?" Barry asked. "Who's working on that for him? A guy named Hunter Zolomon, maybe? A woman named Tina McGee?"

Chyre shook his head. "Naw. I've never seen anyone working on that. I did ask him once. I guess I broke my own rules about questions, right?'" He chuckled, and when no one chuckled along with him, he swallowed his amusement. "I said to him once, 'Hey, boss, half the time I can't even see you when you move. Am I nuts or are you maybe using some kinda speed steroids?'" Chyre licked his lips and uttered a short bark of laughter. "Stupid. Soon as I said it, I thought, *Well, he's gonna off me now.* But he didn't. He just kinda laughed, deep in his throat, and said, 'Call it the power of positive thinking, Fred.'"

Barry did a double take. "That's what he said? The power of positive thinking?"

Chyre shrugged. "Yeah. And then he said, 'I was always

pretty good at math.' And that was it. Never talked to him about it again."

Barry sat back in the chair. What on Earth—any of them—did *that* mean?

20

IRIS WOKE TO THE INSISTENT RING OF a phone. With a sleep-clotted groan, she rolled over and slapped her hand on the nightstand, feeling around until her fingers happened upon the rounded edge of the phone.

When she brought it to her eyes, she realized it was Barry's. At the same time, she realized that the bed was half-empty, Barry's side undisturbed. Exhausted by her day both physically and emotionally, she'd crashed as soon as she'd gotten home. Some part of her hoped that Barry would return as she slept, that she'd wake up with him next to her, safe and warm and so innocent and at peace.

But he was gone, and his phone, left behind when he went to Earth 2, was here in his stead. She stared at it. Was it cool to answer her boyfriend's phone, or was that violating his privacy?

She sneaked a glance at the lock screen. Caller ID read "Frye."

Iris answered. "Mr. Frye?"

There was a pause that, somehow, seemed annoyed. "Who's this?" a gruff voice said.

"I'm Iris. Barry's girlfriend."

Darrel Frye grunted something noncommittal. He was Barry's police union representative, the man charged with helping Barry keep his job.

"Put Allen on," Frye said. "We need to talk."

Iris bit her lip. "Well, he's not around right now."

Another annoyed silence. "Does he plan on being around?"

"I can't really say—"

"He's got a hearing tomorrow. If he wants to keep his job, it might be a good idea to talk to me for five minutes. If he doesn't care, hey—I'll go play golf. Makes no difference to me."

Without so much as a *good-bye*, Frye hung up.

Iris stared at the phone. One day. Barry had only one more day to save his job, and he was nowhere to be found.

Before she could summon up the anger to throw his phone against a wall, *her* phone decided to beep for her attention. It was a text from Cisco:

get to ⚡STAR—got the info you wanted

She rolled out of bed and threw on her clothes.

Wally's first class was at the uncouth hour of 8:30 a.m. He was just dragging himself out of the room when his phone chirped for his attention. He fist-pumped when he saw the text from his sister, telling him to come to S.T.A.R. Labs as soon as possible.

A very cute woman from his Hydrodynamics elective happened to be walking by and smirked at his fist pump. Wally shrugged, abashed, and said, "Uh, I just found out my dad got tickets to the Keystone Jazz Festival."

"Good for your dad," she said.

"Uh, yeah."

As soon as she was out of sight, Wally poured on the speed. He was at S.T.A.R. Labs in three seconds. It took so long only because he detoured to use the bridge rather than run over the river; he didn't want to get his favorite kicks wet.

In the Cortex, H.R. was pouring a cup of coffee for Caitlin while explaining, "This bean, you see, is from Madagascar. The soil there is particularly . . ."

Wally tuned out H.R.'s drone. On the big screen, there was a map of Central City, overlaid with what seemed to be some kind of maze. At various points in the maze, there were glowing red dots.

"What's up?" he asked.

Cisco and Iris sat at the control board. Iris swiveled in her chair while Cisco remained focused on his screen. "A program Cisco set up overnight just finished running. We've got something new in the Earthworm case."

"Oh, joy. More stinky sewer work." Secretly, though, he was pleased. More hero time. More speedster time. *Yes!*

Focusing all of his willpower mightily, he resisted the urge to fist-pump again.

"I had Cisco hack into the Central City Department of Water and Sewage computers," Iris began, "and pull up a schematic of the sewers."

"You know, we throw around this *hacking* pretty casually," H.R. pointed out. "Do you realize Cisco here commits a major felony at least twice a week?"

"All in the name of the greater good," Cisco grumbled. "Get off my back."

"You're mean with no caffeine," H.R. told him. "C'mon. Madagascar Red." He passed the cup under Cisco's nose. "Extremely rare and very expensive, but I have a . . . source."

Cisco inhaled deeply and shuddered in deep pleasure. Then he snapped out of it and shoved H.R. away, almost causing him to spill his precious liquid life. "I'm off that stuff," Cisco remonstrated him. "Possibly for good."

"Heathen! Apostate!" H.R. cried, cradling the cup. "Come to Poppa, baby bean. Don't listen to the mean man . . ."

"Guys," Wally interjected, "I have a thermodynamics class in six minutes. Can we speed things up?"

"Map of the city!" Cisco shouted, pointing. "Overlaid with the sewer system!"

"OK, and . . ."

"And the red dots are where bodies turned up on the surface," Iris said somberly.

Wally whistled. He did a quick count and then, not believing his eyes, counted again. "There's almost a dozen in addition to the two we knew about already. Where—"

"Cops found a third one yesterday afternoon," Iris said. Cisco obligingly sent the victim's info and photo to one of the smaller screens. "Herb Shawn. Found near the museum."

Wally took in the screen quickly, then tracked back to the big screen and found the glowing red dot near the Central City Museum. "OK. What about the rest?"

"Dad came through. Barry had him check out unsolved cases from the past year where organs were removed from the body. In some cases, the victims died of *T. gondii* infestation. In other cases, other complications."

Wally licked his dry lips. "Earthworm is killing people by taking their organs? Gross."

"He's really good at it, too," Caitlin put in. She commandeered another auxiliary screen, and soon a collage of surgical photos appeared. "For a guy performing organ harvesting in a sewer, he does good work. A lot of these people would have survived if they'd been put on proper meds or given follow-up care."

"So . . . Do we think Earthworm doesn't *want* to kill people?" Iris asked.

Wally shook his head. "Doesn't matter. He *is* killing them. We can ask him his intentions after I catch him."

"Which should be a little easier now," Cisco said, gesturing at the big screen. "That 'room' you found in the sewer system is a service node."

"In Central City, the sewer system was designed to also house subterranean electrical cables and storage for the old subway system," Iris added. "There are service nodes like that throughout the tunnels, for when maintenance workers had to access electrical panels and such."

"So now Barry's rubbing off on you and you're an expert on everything, too?" Cisco asked. "Like I was saying: service node!" He panned the image on the big screen, then faded out the city map, leaving the red dots and the sewer schematic. "Notice anything?"

Wally mouthed, *Wow*. It was so obvious now. "All of the bodies were found aboveground, near a service node location. He must use the service nodes to do his meatball surgery and then just toss the victims out of the nearest sewer grate."

"You catch on quick, Kid Flash," Cisco said drily.

"Now you don't have to search the whole tunnel network," Iris told him. "You can focus on these specific areas. We've narrowed it down for you, at least."

Wally hugged her. "Awesome job, Sis!" He spied Cisco over her shoulder. "I would hug you, too, Cisco, but . . . I don't actually want to."

"Am I not lovable?" Cisco pouted until Wally laughed, released Iris, and threw his arms around him.

"Good job, man! Good job."

"I accept your praise and your manly expression of gratitude," Cisco said. "By the time you get back from your class, I'll have some gear whipped up for you, OK?"

Pulling away from Cisco, Wally jittered back and forth, nearly blurring with excitement. "Who can go to class? I wanna go into the tunnels *now*!"

"You promised Dad that being Kid Flash wouldn't interfere with your education," Iris reminded him. "And you'll be better off if you can go with Cisco's equipment. Now get going."

With a protracted and annoyed sigh, Wally dashed off, leaving a momentary wind tunnel in his wake that wrecked everyone's hairstyles.

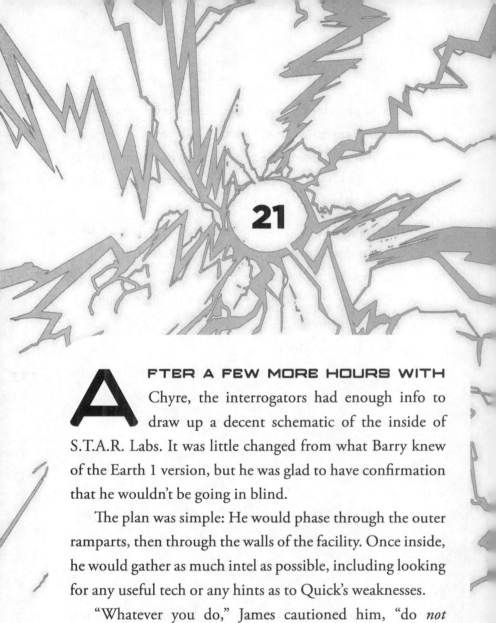

21

AFTER A FEW MORE HOURS WITH Chyre, the interrogators had enough info to draw up a decent schematic of the inside of S.T.A.R. Labs. It was little changed from what Barry knew of the Earth 1 version, but he was glad to have confirmation that he wouldn't be going in blind.

The plan was simple: He would phase through the outer ramparts, then through the walls of the facility. Once inside, he would gather as much intel as possible, including looking for any useful tech or any hints as to Quick's weaknesses.

"Whatever you do," James cautioned him, "do *not* engage him. You're too valuable for us to lose you in a super-speed fight."

It was unnerving, taking orders from the Trickster. But

Barry had to admit he made a lot of sense. Earth 27 was messing with his head something fierce.

With Quick's modifications and fortifications uppermost in his mind, he zoomed off to S.T.A.R. Labs. He dashed through the No-Go Zone so fast that none of the security systems could see him, then vibrated through the rampart. It was thick—more than three feet—the thickest thing he'd ever vibrated through. But he came through on the other side just fine.

The familiar S.T.A.R. Labs complex loomed before him, its silvery exterior patched here and there with black and gold metallic plates. Repairs from the explosion, no doubt. He ran toward the building, zipped up the side of one of the towers, and phased through a second-floor wall.

According to Chyre's memory, there would be an elevator near here that would take him belowground to the sublevels. Barry had his first moment of panic and distrust when he didn't see the elevator where it should have been. But then he peeked around a corner and there it was—on the opposite side of the wall as the same spot on Earth 1.

Waiting for the elevator to come was torturous. By his internal count, it took only a few seconds, but they ticked down like hours to him. He was painfully aware of how alone he was. Usually, he had Cisco's or Caitlin's reassuring voice in his ear when he was Flash-ing around. Right now, he had no one but himself.

And that'll be enough, Allen.

The elevator doors slid open and he went inside. Another agonizing wait.

Sublevel 3 of the Earth 1 S.T.A.R. Labs housed Dr. Wells's personal workshop and storage for spare parts. Here, it held . . . well, no one knew. The area was off-limits even to Johnny Quick's most trusted lieutenants. Which meant the Rogues desperately wanted to know what was there.

There were no lights when the elevator doors opened, only the spill of illumination from the elevator itself. Barry stepped into the darkness, senses on high alert. He couldn't just race around in the dark; he had to be careful.

As the doors slid shut, crushing the light into nothingness, he felt around for a light switch on the wall.

Zip. Zilch. Nada.

Maybe the lights were voice-activated. He wasn't going to try shouting into the void, though.

The Rogues had given him a camera and some gear, including a very small, very weak flashlight. It was important to fly under the radar, so he couldn't be throwing around a laser light or ostentatious LED.

Playing the light along the floor, he saw a layer of dust.

When was the last time anyone had been down here? How important could it be if no one ever came here?

He crept forward, following his beam. There didn't seem to be a corridor here—it seemed like one big chamber.

Almost tripping, he noticed a thick cable pulled taut along the floor. Some exploration with the flashlight revealed further cables, all of them leading in the same direction: toward the center of the chamber.

Following them, he heard something. A gurgle, almost. Maybe a drip . . . ? Not water, though. Something thicker. Heavier.

The cables led to a podium of sorts that seemed to grow up out of the floor. Just beyond it was a tall cylinder. Painted a matte black, it blended into the murk, effectively invisible.

Barry danced his light beam over the cylinder, finding no seams or connections. It stretched from floor to ceiling, nine or ten feet tall, and to Barry's trained eye had a diameter of approximately six feet. The podium was a control panel of some sort. He ran his hands over it, carefully not pressing anything.

Take some pictures. Take some pictures and then go scout the rest of the facility.

But he couldn't resist. The podium's proximity to the

cylinder meant the two had to be connected. And the drip-ping, gurgling sound was definitely coming from inside the cylinder.

He could have phased through it, but who knew what was in there?

He studied the control panel. Nothing was labeled. There was a lever and some buttons, as well as a numerical keypad.

Licking his lips, he reached for the lever. If anything weird happened, he would shove it back into place at super-speed.

He eased the lever out of position. As he did so, the cyl-inder made a slight, almost inaudible grinding noise. The shell of it turned the tiniest bit, and a slice of watery light spilled out.

He pushed the lever farther. The shell of the cylinder finished rotating, folding back into itself, revealing a trans-parent tube, filled with some kind of translucent, viscous fluid. Floating within was a figure. A man. He was naked, tethered by electrodes on his scalp and under his arms, the wires snaking up to the ceiling. An oxygen mask was fitted over his face. His head was shaved.

Johnny Quick. Is this how he boosts his speed?

Almost as soon as the thought came to him, he dismissed

it. Drifting in the liquid, the man, who was unconscious or asleep, turned just a tad in some invisible current as the cylinder thrummed. Barry saw his face full-on and recognized him, even with the oxygen mask obscuring the lower half of his face.

Clyde Mardon!

No sooner had he thought it than his eyesight went blank for a moment. The room filled with bright light, blinding him. Barry put his hands up to shield his eyes, but popping bubbles of brightness assaulted his vision.

"Welcome," said a throaty voice, and Barry turned, rapidly blinking to clear his vision, and saw none other than Johnny Quick.

The costume was just barely similar enough to his own that it almost felt like looking in a mirror. Johnny Quick's red was a little brighter and his lightning motif more ostentatious, double bolts striking down from his shoulders to meet in a V at his waist. Two bolts jutted from his cowl, poking up and out in a manner that seemed threatening.

The cowl itself did not cover his eyes, but it didn't matter. He was using the same face-blurring speed trick that Barry often used, turning his features into a smear of shimmering color, an indistinct blob.

"When my men told me there was someone with super-speed in the city," Quick said, his voice vibrating, "I confess, I didn't believe them. And yet here you are." He paused for just an instant. "Nice costume."

Barry was keenly aware that Quick could charge at him at any instant. For that matter, Barry could do the same in reverse, which Quick had to know. They were at a stalemate, each of them too aware of the other's speed. He said nothing, watching for an opening, a momentary distraction. He would need less than a second to cross the floor and knock out Quick.

"So, you idiots finally kidnapped Chyre," Quick mused. "I hope you didn't torture him too much—he was told to mouth off after a little pressure. Just to make it believable."

"You wanted us to catch him?"

Johnny Quick tsked. "Of course I did. You think I was just going to wait here in my bunker for the statues to figure out how to get in? So much easier to tell them how to get in, so that they do it on my schedule, where and when I want them to. Makes it simple to catch them—actually, *you*—in the act. Not much of a tactical thinker, are you? That's the problem with people with powers—they let the powers do all the work." Quick tapped a finger against his skull. "Gotta use the ol' bean."

Barry cleared his throat. "You don't have tech that controls the weather. You've just got Clyde Mardon hooked up to some kind of brain wave manipulator so that you can use *his* power. On my Earth, he was evil, so I bet here he was good."

"Clyde Mardon? Is *that* his name?" Johnny Quick shrugged. "I don't know what this 'my Earth' nonsense is, but, yeah, he was a real do-gooder. A lot like him out there. Most of them, we get rid of. Usually we just eliminate the hyper-powered as soon as they manifest. But his powers . . ." Quick sighed a vibrating sigh. "His powers were just too useful to let molder in a grave somewhere. So I hooked him up to this machinery, and now his powers—and the weather—are mine to control. What a terrific way to keep people in line. Protesters start lining up? Hit 'em with a downpour. People getting annoyed? Crippling heat wave. So, yeah, he does my bidding, and in return he gets . . ." Johnny contemplated. "Well, he doesn't get killed. That's not a bad reward."

As he finished speaking, Johnny Quick tilted his head down the slightest bit and chuckled. For an instant, his attention was diverted from Barry, and Barry took advantage, accelerating from a dead stop to Mach 2 in the space of two steps. He was on Quick before the man could look up and lashed out with a brutal haymaker at the other speedster's jaw.

But Johnny feinted left at the last possible millisecond, and Barry's fist missed by a whisker. Quick super-sped to the other end of the room.

"Now, was that polite?" he asked in a tone of mock sincerity. "I was making pleasant conversation and you assaulted me."

Barry clenched his fists. "I don't know how you handle them, but where I come from, we don't cotton to dictators."

He expected outrage, but Johnny Quick merely laughed. "That doesn't seem very practical. I suppose in an abstract way, a dictatorship could be seen as less than ideal for, say, the statues. But think about it: If you don't have powers and your overlord does, what's the point in rebelling? You'll lose every time. Better to know your place, keep your head down, and thank your superiors for your continued existence."

"What about equality? What about democracy?" Barry fumed.

"Overrated," Quick said with a yawn. "Obsolete in the age of the hyperhuman."

Hyperhuman. The Earth 27 word for *metahuman*, no doubt.

Quick stepped to his left. Barry shadowed him. There was only ten feet of empty floor between them; it would take a fraction of a second for Barry to close the distance. But in that same fraction, Quick would evade.

"When you have a class of beings so dramatically and obviously superior," Johnny Quick went on, "there's no point in indulging in the comforting fiction that we were all created equal."

They paced around each other, two prizefighters sizing each other up, waiting patiently for an opening. Zoom had been aggressive and brutal; the Reverse-Flash had been in love with his own speed.

Johnny Quick was thoughtful. Willing to wait.

"Why not use your powers to protect the weak?" Barry asked. "Be a hero, not a tyrant."

Quick shook his head. "What a naive proposition. Strength leads to fear, which leads to compliance. Does anything else matter?"

"There's a different way."

"Oh? Where's your proof?"

In another universe, Barry had to admit. From what he'd seen of Earth 27, heroism didn't seem to function all that well. Was it that evil got in a foothold early on, or was there just something fundamentally broken in this universe?

"People like us live by different rules," Johnny said. "Different rules of morality, different rules of society. Heck, different rules of *physics*! Surely you see that. You can't possibly think that the same guidelines and regulations that govern the statues should apply to us, can you?"

Through gritted teeth, Barry said, "Stop. Calling them. Statues."

Quick laughed. "Don't be so offended on their behalf. Think it through. Imagine yourself at my side. The one thing that has held me back so far is that even I can't be in more than one place at a time. With you on my team, we would be unstoppable. Superwoman, Ultraman, the others . . . They wouldn't stand a chance against us. You and I could expand beyond Central City and take the entire world!"

Barry pretended to consider this. He needed to catch Quick off guard, he realized. They were too evenly matched in speed. If he could make Quick drop his defenses, though, maybe there would be an opening . . .

"It's not the worst idea I've ever heard," Barry told him. "But how could I trust you not to double-cross me once I helped you eliminate the other meta—I mean, the other hyperhumans?"

Johnny chortled. "See? You already think like I do! I love that! I'll give you an honest answer: You can't trust me. I mean, I'll be happy ruling half of the world and letting you have the other half, but, yeah, you can't be sure of that. Then again, I also can't be sure that *you* won't betray *me*.

We'll both have unlimited resources and our own powers. You just have to believe in yourself, believe that you will be able to defend what's yours." He shrugged. "I believe that of myself. I believe it enough to extend a hand of partnership and cooperation to you."

And he literally held out his hand.

This was Barry's chance. Moving at perfectly normal, human, nonthreatening speed, he approached Johnny Quick and clasped his hand. This close, the vibrating face was unnerving, a staticky, amorphous blot.

"All right, you've got a deal. We'll work together." He needed another moment, another instant for Johnny to become relaxed enough to let his guard down completely. "Just answer one question for me: How did you get your speed?" Barry asked, not expecting an answer.

To his surprise, though, Quick responded as they shook hands. "Sheer chance. I was in the lab at CCPD the night the particle accelerator blew. A lightning bolt came through the skylight and shattered a rack of chemicals, dousing me. Somehow, the combination of chemicals and electricity—"

"Gave you superspeed," Barry whispered.

Quick laughed. "No! Don't be ridiculous. That would be absurd. What it did was . . . open my mind, let's say. Show me a path to the speed. So . . . How did you get *your* speed?"

Barry swallowed as he released Johnny Quick's hand.

Because the answer was close enough to be the same. Now he knew who Johnny Quick was.

He was Barry.

Ralph Dibny had said Johnny Quick seemed like a cop. Snart had said flat out that Quick looked and sounded like Barry. The clues had been there all along, and he'd conveniently ignored them.

There'd been no grave for Barry Allen in the Earth 27 cemetery, and now he knew why. Just as Captain Cold and Heat Wave and the other Rogues were good guys in this universe, Barry himself was a villain. And not just *any* villain: a deluded, murderous despot who ruled Central City with an iron fist and worked in concert with other psychopaths to keep the world in a state of constant terror. The worst possible version of himself.

The moment had passed. He'd paused just too long, and now any answer he gave to Quick's question would be suspect. Everything was off-kilter, and Quick knew it. His posture changed, and Barry knew that in an instant, Johnny Quick would strike.

So Barry struck first, throwing a right jab, followed by a left cross. A simple boxing combination Joe had taught him as a kid, something to keep the bullies at bay. Right-left. Boom, boom. Easy as pie.

Johnny avoided the jab, but the cross caught him in the

jaw and sent him staggering backward, colliding against the wall. Barry advanced at top speed, throwing a left hook, but Quick phased and ducked at the same time, skittering right through Barry, whose momentum carried him into the wall.

He spun around, too late—Quick was already on him, snarling, a red-clad fist crashing down on Barry. His head snapped back and slammed into the wall again—and not for the first time, he silently thanked Cisco for the shock-absorption layer built into his cowl. It was as thin as fabric but as sturdy as a motorcycle helmet, and it had saved him from a concussion more than once.

Like now. He was rattled but not knocked out. He ducked under another punch and aimed an uppercut at Quick's solar plexus.

But Quick moved at the last possible nanosecond, and the blow caught him on the side instead. Quick hissed in a painful breath, but he didn't have the wind knocked out of him. He was still standing.

They raced toward each other, the room filling with the crackle and sizzle of electricity. Red-and-yellow lightning arced and spat into the air, and the room grew hotter and soon stank of ozone.

They were too evenly matched, two speedsters with equal speed. And they were, after all, the same man. Two Barry Allens, mirror images in conflict. For every speedy punch and kick, there was an equally fast dodge or feint. It was the meeting of two objects of equal mass and velocity in the rare case of a perfectly elastic collision. Neither of them could gain the upper hand. Barry couldn't lose, but he couldn't win, either.

Quick ran up the wall and kicked off the ceiling, launching himself like a human missile at Barry. Barry pivoted aside and lashed out with his fist, catching Quick in the side. Quick cried out and rolled away, then sprang up on his feet and whipped twin whirlwinds into existence, aiming them squarely at Barry.

For the first time in his life, Barry was on the receiving end of the old "spin your arms to make cyclones" trick. And it *sucked*. Gasping for breath, he was knocked backward several feet, crashing into another wall.

They volleyed back and forth like that for several more seconds, their combat abbreviated due to their speed. It had been less than a minute and they'd already traded hundreds of blows and kicks. Now they backed off, once again circling each other, both of them breathing hard.

The vibrating splotch of Johnny Quick's face did not move, but Barry thought he heard something nonetheless. "What did you say?"

There was a cruel glee in Quick's voice when he responded: "Nothing you need concern yourself with." And then he moved.

Fast.

Too fast. Faster than he had before. Faster than Barry.

Before he could react, Barry felt the punches, three of them aligned along his rib cage. He cried out and fell back, only to have his head grabbed and slammed into Quick's knee. Johnny Quick was so fast that Barry saw only a blur broken by moments of darkness as fists pummeled him. This must be how other people saw *him*. He suddenly felt a wave of sympathy for all the bad guys he'd coldcocked at the speed of sound. *This* was what it felt like.

Staggering backward, he stumbled into the cylinder that held Clyde Mardon in suspension. Johnny Quick grabbed him and threw him across the room, then zipped to his side and kicked him in the ribs before he could pick himself up off the floor.

"Not as fast as you think you are, eh?" Quick sneered.

"How . . . How can you . . ." Barry's words came out slurred, his mouth numb with pain.

"My speed mantra," Johnny Quick crowed. "Focuses me. Gives me a greater connection to HyperHeaven. Makes me fast enough to do *this*."

Barry didn't even see the next four or five punches. They came at him so fast that they seemed to meld into a single punishing blast of agony. His mouth tasted like burnt steel and blood. Teeth rattled.

Then, with a cry of triumph, Quick hauled Barry to his feet. He pinned Barry to the wall with his left forearm and ripped off his cowl with his right hand.

"Who are—" Even through the blur of speed, Barry could tell that Quick's eyes widened in shock.

"Barry Allen?" the other speedster whispered. "You're *Barry Allen*? How is that even possible? You . . . I . . ."

In Johnny Quick's moment of frozen surprise, Barry managed to wrench himself free. Groaning in pain, he forced himself to run, dashing across the room and vibrating through the wall. He faltered on his way through, tripping over his own feet and almost collapsing as he emerged on the other side, but the certain knowledge that Johnny Quick was right behind him spurred him on. He turned to the left and vanished through that wall, too, then kept going, making random turns and phasing through random walls, trying to put as much solid, opaque matter between him and the other speedster as possible.

Discretion is the better part of valor echoed in his mind. Joe had taught him that, too, along with the boxing lessons.

I'm teaching you how to defend yourself, Joe had said, *because I want you to stand up when you have to. But I also don't want you to be stupid, you hear me? If you're outnumbered, you don't take a stand. You run. Hear me? You* run, *Barry. Run.*

"I hear you, Joe," Barry croaked, and kept running.

On a panic-spiked adrenaline high, Barry could have run halfway to Coast City, but instead he found himself weaving through the streets of Central City, reeling from avenue to avenue, boulevard to boulevard. Rain started, then changed to sleet, then to hard, driving hail. The few people outside rushed for cover. Barry batted hailstones out of his way and thought of Clyde Mardon, hooked up like a spare hard drive to his doppelgänger's machinery, made to manipulate the weather so that Johnny Quick could slow Barry down and catch him.

Can't let him. Can't let him get me. Too fast. He's too fast.

Barry ducked into an alleyway off to his left. He slipped on a spread of hailstones the size of marbles and with the slickness of ice, losing his balance. Coming down hard on already-bruised ribs, he slid the length of the alley and collided with a brick wall.

Don't pass out, he thought fiercely. *Stay alert. Don't pass—*

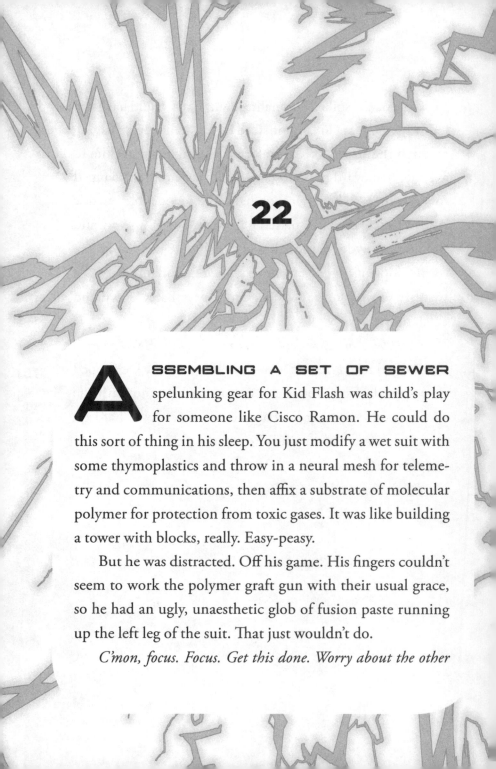

22

ASSEMBLING A SET OF SEWER spelunking gear for Kid Flash was child's play for someone like Cisco Ramon. He could do this sort of thing in his sleep. You just modify a wet suit with some thymoplastics and throw in a neural mesh for telemetry and communications, then affix a substrate of molecular polymer for protection from toxic gases. It was like building a tower with blocks, really. Easy-peasy.

But he was distracted. Off his game. His fingers couldn't seem to work the polymer graft gun with their usual grace, so he had an ugly, unaesthetic glob of fusion paste running up the left leg of the suit. That just wouldn't do.

C'mon, focus. Focus. Get this done. Worry about the other

stuff later. Plenty of time to stress after you've finished Wally's suit.

He scraped the paste off and tried again. This time, he managed to draw a perfect bead of fusion paste along the polymer seam; it welded the two plastic surfaces together with an almost invisible joint. Very nice.

He sighed in relief and allowed himself a moment to close his eyes. There was just too much going on. Too much of everything. A freak named Earthworm with a body count they hadn't even nailed down yet. Hocus Pocus and his freaky techno-magic, complete with a locked room escape for the ages. And then poor Barry, off somewhere in the multiverse thanks to a busted tachyon harness. Cisco wished he could just vibe himself somewhere calm and quiet and pleasant and uncomplicated . . .

"Hey! Who are *you*?" a familiar voice said.

He opened his eyes and on the other side of the workbench saw . . .

Himself.

He was looking into the eyes of Cisco Ramon.

"Oh, this is freaky," he said. He was vibing, he realized, but not intentionally. He'd somehow been pulled into a vibe against his will, without touching anything special or focusing his power. It was as though the vibe itself called to him.

Freaky, yeah, but Cisco knew that the Multiverse contained, well, multitudes. Hence the name. He was obviously looking at the Cisco from another Earth.

"You can't be my Earth 2 version," the other Cisco said slowly. "He died. What Earth are you from?"

Cisco tilted his head. This made no sense. Yes, his Earth 2 version—the evil Vibe—had died during their pursuit of Zoom many months ago. But how could *this* Cisco know that? Unless . . . Had this Cisco made contact with Earth 2 before Team Flash had? Things were getting confusing, even more confusing than usual when it came to traversing the dimensions of the Multiverse.

There was one way to clear it up: "I'm from Earth 1," Cisco said. "What about you?"

The other Cisco narrowed his eyes in suspicion. "No. *I'm* from Earth 1."

"Well, then, amigo, we have a little problem, 'cause you're looking at the one and only Francisco Ramon of Earth Uno," Cisco said with a bravado he did not entirely feel.

"I beg to differ," the other replied. "*I'm* the one and only, et cetera."

They frowned identical frowns at each other for a moment and then—at the same time—said, "Time travel!"

"One of us is from the future—"

"—and one of us is from the past," Cisco finished for him. "What year is it for you?"

The other Cisco told him, and *Yikes!* It was the same year for Cisco. When they compared months and days, they were identical. Down to the hour.

"This is impossible," the other Cisco said. "Maybe you just use a different numbering system for your Earths. Can you describe Earth 1?"

Cisco was tempted to say *big, blue, round,* but the other Cisco said, "And describe it *without* saying *big, blue, and round.*"

So Cisco rattled off key facts, including the details of the particle accelerator explosion. The more he spoke, the more the other Cisco seemed confused and disturbed.

"Who was in charge of your particle accelerator?" he asked.

Now Cisco began to worry—what if this *other Cisco* was actually a shape-shifter? Or an illusion cast by an enemy? Someone trying to get intel on Team Flash?

"Who was in charge of *your* particle accelerator?" he challenged.

The other Cisco frowned, and Cisco knew exactly what he was thinking: Shape-shifter. Illusion. Someone trying to get intel . . .

"We're not going to get anywhere fighting each other," the other Cisco said. "How about we count to three and then say who was in charge of the accelerator?"

"'Three shall be the number thou shalt count, and the number of the counting shall be three,'" Cisco said in a British falsetto.

"I knew you would go *Holy Grail* on me," the other Cisco said with grudging admiration. "One . . ."

"Two . . ."

"Three!"

"Reverse-Flash disguised as Harrison Wells!" they both shouted at the same time.

And then just . . . stared at each other for a long, long time.

"I don't get it," Cisco said after a moment. As far as he knew, there was only one Reverse-Flash, only one universe in which Eobard Thawne, lost in his own past, had killed and then replaced Dr. Wells. And that was on Earth 1. *This* Earth. "We can't be the same person. Can we? Could we really be vibing ourself?" Was this whole exchange some kind of bizarre metahuman mirror trick? Was his unconscious breaking down, leaking his powers everywhere?

The other Cisco seemed just as concerned. "I don't know. That sounds . . . weird. Tell me something about you. Anything."

And that Star City concert popped back into Cisco's head, entirely unbidden. He recounted it to the other Cisco, who nodded along, clearly recalling the exact same story. But there was something off in the other Cisco. A sadness lurked in his eyes and at the corners of his mouth as Cisco told the story of his trip with Dante.

"It was a great day," Cisco said, finishing. "He actually treated me like his brother, not—"

"—his burden." The other Cisco wiped his eyes. "Yeah, I remember."

Cisco couldn't figure out why his doppelgänger was so lachrymose at the thought of Dante. "But things are a lot better now," he said. "We're in a better place now. We get along, and it's kinda . . ."

The other Cisco stared at him in silence for a moment. "Oh my God," he breathed. "You're from Flashpoint!"

"Wait, what's Flashpoint?"

The other Cisco waved him quiet for a moment. "You said the year was . . . and that would mean . . ." He nodded to himself. "And you said your Earth 2 doppelgänger is dead. So you've been to Earth 2 and you fought Zoom—"

"And kicked his speedy butt into the Speed Force. Yeah. So?"

"And right after that . . . You all went to Joe West's house to celebrate, right? But Barry left partway through."

"No."

"What do you mean, *no*?"

"Uh, it's not a complicated word. No, as in: negatory. Not. Uh-uh. As in: Barry didn't leave the party."

"He had to. That's when he went back in time and created Flashpoint."

"Dude, he stepped outside for, like, a second. Iris went out and talked to him, and next thing I knew, they came back inside, and that was it. He was with us the rest of the night."

The other Cisco fell mute.

"Seriously, what's a *Flashpoint*?" Cisco asked. "Sounds like Barry doing his best 'Stayin' Alive' dance moves."

The other Cisco gnawed at his knuckle, deep in thought. "Flashpoint is . . . was . . . I don't even know the right tense for it. Barry went back in time and stopped Reverse-Flash from killing his mother."

Cisco shook his head. "No. No, he didn't. Didn't happen."

The other Cisco held up a hand. "Let me finish. That created an alternate timeline, called Flashpoint. But then . . ." He sighed. "There's too much to go into. Things went wrong—Kid Flash died and the Rival was making trouble in Central City, so Barry went back *again* and stopped himself from changing history, and *your* timeline got wiped out and replaced with ours. With a timeline where Dante *died*. But he's still alive in your timeline because you're in Flashpoint. Which shouldn't even exist anymore."

The other Cisco seemed so distraught and confused that Cisco hated to pile on, but he had no choice. "Um, I don't know how to break it to you, but Kid Flash is just fine here. And I don't know who 'the Rival' is. We're not in this Flashpoint thingy you keep mentioning."

"But that's imposs—"

"Like I said before: Barry didn't go back in time that night to change history. He never did. So I live in—"

"My God . . . !" The other Cisco snapped his fingers. "A third timeline! There's my timeline, there's Flashpoint, and there's yours, the timeline that would have existed if Barry never went back in time in the first place!"

Cisco grunted and frowned. He didn't like his doppelgänger's attitude. "Um, I'm not in the third timeline, champ. I'm in the *first*. The original. The one that is supposed to exist because Barry didn't meddle. Flashpoint and wherever you live—those are divergent timelines, branching off of mine."

The other Cisco laughed without mirth. "No, no. Mine is the core timeline. Everything originated there."

"No, it's like branches of a tree. We share the same trunk."

The other Cisco shrugged. "So, now what? Is this like living in another parallel universe?"

Cisco stroked his chin. "I don't think so. Parallel universes like Earth 2 and Earth 3 developed at the same time as Earth 1. They 'grew up' together, in parallel. This is more like . . . divergent universes. Like the distributaries in some rivers."

"There must be something special about Earth 1," the other Cisco mused, "for it to be able to split itself like this. Zoom said that Earth 1 was the foundation of the Multiverse. So maybe it can handle being splintered into different timelines."

Cisco felt a chill run up his spine and spread along his entire back and shoulders. This just felt WRONG. Plain WRONG.

"We're not going to get anywhere philosophizing about this," Cisco said. "We're the only ones who know about this. Part of our power is the ability to remember discarded timelines. Like when Reverse-Flash killed us with the ol' vibrating-hand-in-the-heart, but then Barry changed time and we were alive again. So only you and I know about Earth 1 and . . . let's call it Earth 1A."

As soon as he said it, he realized how uncomfortable it made him. Was it right for something so huge to be only in HIS mind?

"I see where you're going with this," the other Cisco said grimly.

"Yeah. What do we *do* about it?"

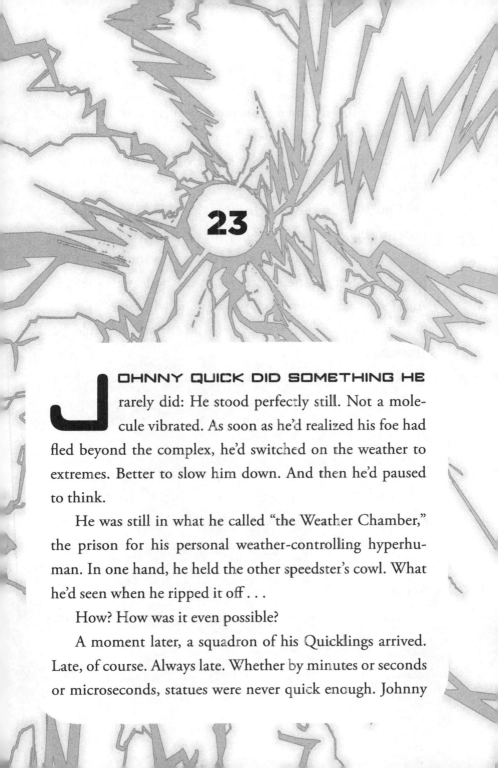

23

JOHNNY QUICK DID SOMETHING HE
rarely did: He stood perfectly still. Not a mole-
cule vibrated. As soon as he'd realized his foe had
fled beyond the complex, he'd switched on the weather to
extremes. Better to slow him down. And then he'd paused
to think.

He was still in what he called "the Weather Chamber,"
the prison for his personal weather-controlling hyperhuman. In one hand, he held the other speedster's cowl. What
he'd seen when he ripped it off . . .

How? How was it even possible?

A moment later, a squadron of his Quicklings arrived.
Late, of course. Always late. Whether by minutes or seconds
or microseconds, statues were never quick enough. Johnny

Quick waited for them constantly, precious milliseconds evaporated by their tardiness.

"Sir!" the captain of the squadron called. "What are your orders?"

Quick finally moved. He lifted the cowl to his face, staring at it. Impossible. Absolutely impossible, what he'd seen.

"Find him," Quick said. "Fan out. I want every street patrolled, every gutter searched, every building explored. And I want it done so quickly that even *I* will think it's fast."

"Sir, we don't have any imagery of him. He could be anyone—"

Quick thrust the cowl at the captain. "He's wearing a costume that matches *this*, you dolt!"

The captain swallowed hard. "But, sir, he could have changed clothes—"

Johnny Quick began vibrating so fast that the air for ten feet around him buzzed and threw off sparks. "Then pretend he's Cinderella and go door-to-door until you find the man who fits this cowl! You've already wasted three whole seconds!" Quick screamed, his thunderous, bombinating voice filling the chamber with harsh echoes. "Go!"

They scrambled over one another to get out of the room. It still took too long.

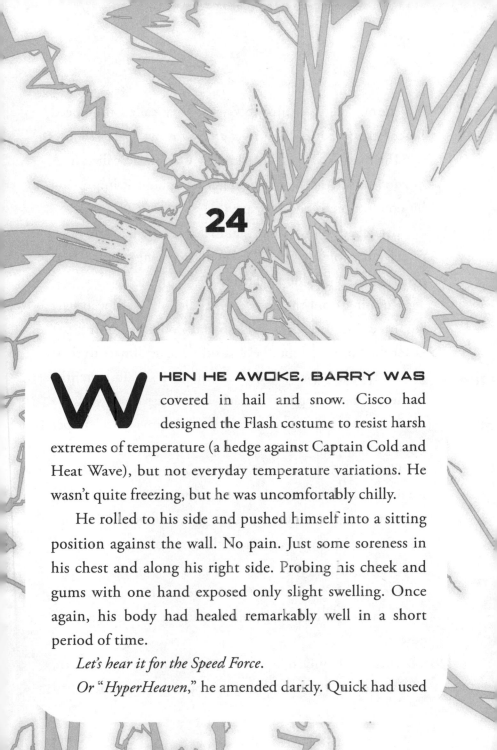

24

WHEN HE AWOKE, BARRY WAS covered in hail and snow. Cisco had designed the Flash costume to resist harsh extremes of temperature (a hedge against Captain Cold and Heat Wave), but not everyday temperature variations. He wasn't quite freezing, but he was uncomfortably chilly.

He rolled to his side and pushed himself into a sitting position against the wall. No pain. Just some soreness in his chest and along his right side. Probing his cheek and gums with one hand exposed only slight swelling. Once again, his body had healed remarkably well in a short period of time.

Let's hear it for the Speed Force.

Or "HyperHeaven," he amended darkly. Quick had used

that term. That was probably what they called the Speed Force here on Earth 27. *Vive la différence.*

The mantra. That's what Johnny Quick had called it. A *speed mantra.* And he'd said something about it improving his connection to HyperHeaven.

Barry had to figure out that mantra. If he had any hope of defeating Johnny Quick, it lay in becoming just as fast as his cruel Earth 27 doppelgänger.

Running from the amped-up Quick, he had been—he admitted—scared. Reverse-Flash and Zoom had both been faster than him, too, but he'd had time to acclimate to their greater speeds. Johnny Quick's mantra kicked in instantly, in the middle of a fight, and Barry had gone from having the upper hand to being punched in the face with Quick's upper hand. Repeatedly. Ow.

He wasn't scared now. No. He was *angry.* At himself. The Rogues and all the decent people of Earth 27 were counting on him, whether they knew it or not, and so shame conjoined with his anger, the two emotions roiling like a toxic stew in his gut.

He wouldn't return to the Rogues without something more than a hangdog expression and a tale of his own defeat.

There was only one other place to go on this Earth, and so he went there. The impromptu winter storm had blown over (been shut off by Clyde Mardon, more likely) and Quicklings were out in force, marching in the streets, columns of them in lockstep next to slow-moving tanks. A manhunt. For him.

He ran up the side of a building, vaulted himself over the balustrade at the top, and sped across the roof, moving so fast that with a single bound, his momentum carried him over the gap to the next building. In this manner, he made his way across the city, to the cluster of buildings that sandwiched in Madame Xanadu's shop. The Quicklings were marching here, too, so Barry waited for a gap in their formation and hustled through to the door at superspeed.

As always, it took his eyes time to adjust to the half-light of Madame Xanadu's shop. When they did, he realized that she had company: Sitting across from her at her table was a tall, broad-shouldered man in a suit so deeply blue it seemed black. He wore a cloak in the same color, as well as a fedora. From this angle, Barry could see wisps of shock-white hair peeking out from under the hat.

Barry paused, his back to the closed front door, and waited politely, not wishing to interfere. Madame Xanadu and the man huddled close together, murmuring to each other over the table. At one point, the man glanced back at Barry, the brim of his hat casting a shadow over his eyes so that Barry could not tell if they evinced recognition, worry, aggression . . . anything at all. Under the suit, Barry saw now, the man wore a white turtleneck and a pendant.

After a few moments, the two of them finished their conversation. The man stood and, with a flourish of his cape, disappeared through the curtain into the back of the shop. Barry had a nagging feeling that the man had disappeared from more than just the front room.

"I didn't mean to intrude on you and your friend," he said, sliding into the now-vacated chair.

Madame Xanadu tilted her head to one side, her expression neutral. "He is no friend of mine. He is a stranger."

"Like me, then."

She smiled. "I don't consider you a stranger. Not anymore. Not after what we've been through."

"Friends, then?"

For a moment, she considered this. "There is a spectrum between friend and stranger. We lie somewhere on it, at neither pole."

"Too bad. I could use a friend on this Earth." Without meaning to, he told her everything—his encounter with the Rogues, his meeting with James Jesse, his infiltration of S.T.A.R. Labs. And everything that had transpired thereafter, including his humiliating defeat at the hands of Earth 27's version of himself.

"Gives new meaning to the phrase *Don't beat yourself up*, doesn't it?" he cracked mordantly.

Steepling her fingers in front of herself, she bore such a resemblance to her Earth 1 self that Barry felt a strong pang of homesickness. "You blame yourself for not knowing something you could not know."

"I should have predicted that I was Johnny Quick. It seems so obvious."

"In retrospect, many things are obvious. Hindsight makes sages of fools and geniuses of the oblivious." Her blue eyes sparkled. "Every moment that passes, we become new people, accruing new experiences, new information, new contexts. Why maltreat yourself for not being the person you are *now* an hour ago? Will you similarly berate yourself an hour hence for the person you are now as you sit with me?"

Barry mulled that over. It sounded an awful lot like a fancy way of saying *Don't beat yourself up*, and he wasn't sure he bought it.

"I let everyone down," he told her. "They needed me to get information, and I blew it. And on top of that, I'll never get home."

"It seems to me you succeeded. You *did* acquire information, after all. You now know who Johnny Quick is and how he enhances his speed. This is information. Quite valuable, I would imagine."

True. Why, he wondered, had the Earth 27 version of himself taken on the name *Johnny Quick*? Maybe that mattered. Maybe if the Rogues knew the true name of their tyrant, it would offer a key to defeating him.

"As to going home, well . . ." She shrugged. "You know better than most that across the length and breadth of the universes, there are myriad possibilities and potentialities. After such a short time here, are you already ready to give up?"

Was he?

No. No, of course not. Giving up meant sitting still and surrendering. He was the Flash. He *moved*. That's what he did.

"Just telling the Rogues that they're up against a former CSI named Barry Allen isn't going to help," he told her, leaning forward earnestly. "Nor is telling them that he has a speed mantra. I need to know what that mantra is. So that I can figure out how to counter it."

"In that specific instance, I believe I can help you."

Madame Xanadu removed one of her rings and held it between her thumb and forefinger, about a foot from Barry's eyes. The ring was bulky, of white gold, with a shiny black stone.

He knew how hypnosis worked. As a kid, he'd been fascinated by it and had read voraciously on the subject. Joe and Iris had both kindly indulged his obsession, agreeing to sit for endless-seeming hours as he spun shiny tops or pendulumed necklaces before them, intoning, "You are getting sleeeeeeeepy," over and over, all for naught. Though his knowledge was deep (for an eleven-year-old), his hypnotic prowess was nil.

Hypnosis was essentially a state of suggestibility. In a nutshell, it bypassed the conscious mind and accessed the part of the brain used while dreaming. Since the conscious mind had all sorts of filters in place, bypassing it allowed the subject to think and remember in an unencumbered fashion, sending information and memories right to the surface without the self-censoring influence of the waking mind.

In theory, hypnosis allowed the subject to focus his or her memory on fine-grained details that the conscious mind had either ignored or filtered out. In practice, it worked . . . sometimes.

He stared at the ring. This was a hypnotic induction technique called *Braidism*, named for the guy who invented it. It boiled down to this: You get someone like Barry to stare at an object at just the right distance (like, say, a shiny ring a foot away). The eyes focus exclusively on that object, staring at it, and thinking only of it. Eventually, this causes a response in the subject's pupils, which dilate. And then the eyes close entirely and the subject is under.

Barry knew the theory a little too well. It was easy enough to keep his eyes locked on the ring, much harder to keep his mind from wandering through the corridors of knowledge on hypnosis. Ironically, thinking about hypnosis was keeping him from being hypnotized.

"The ring's stone is black," Madame Xanadu said in a monotone. "It is featureless, a void. Stare into it."

He locked his gaze on the stone. Images swam in there, murky and indistinct. Chiseled from fog and swaddled in darkness. He stared at them as they shifted and shivered into new shapes, dissolving and dispersing before he could identify them. The ring seemed to grow, to expand until it filled the entirety of his vision. At same time, Madame Xanadu continued speaking in that soothing, lulling monotone.

He did not realize he was in a trance when it happened; that would have defeated the purpose and snapped him out of it. More, he *accepted* that he was already in a trance, his eyes fluttering closed, hearing only Madame Xanadu's voice.

"You are in the tyrant's complex," she told him with tranquil composure. "You see him before you."

Barry did just that. Without opening his eyes, without moving a muscle, he was back in S.T.A.R. Labs, standing next to Clyde Mardon's cylindrical prison-*cum*-medical berth, watching Johnny Quick at the other end of the room.

"He's in front of me," Barry said, his own voice slow and dreamlike. "I see him."

"Find that moment where he spoke his mantra. Focus on it. Relive it, only this time slowly."

The moments skipped past him at a speed even *he* thought to be fast. Almost instantly, he recognized that time when Quick had recited his mantra. He slowed down the memory.

He saw and realized what he'd seen and *not* realized in the heat of the battle: When Johnny Quick had lowered his head to speak his mantra, he'd been so focused on the mantra that for a moment his face had stopped vibrating. It was an odd angle, but . . .

"I see his lips moving."

"Can you hear him?"

"Yes. Barely. *Three*."

"Go on."

Barry furrowed his brow. He could hear Quick, yes, but so faintly. He needed the visual of the moving lips, too, to solidify what he was hearing.

Three, Johnny said.

Ex.

And then *to*.

"Three ex to," Madame Xanadu repeated, and Barry realized he was speaking Quick's words aloud. "Continue. What else? Three ex to what?"

Beads of sweat popped free on Barry's forehead as he drilled deep into the memory.

Three ex to . . .

And then a whole snatch of a phrase: *The quantity nine why zee.*

Watching Quick's lips form the syllables. The upper teeth dragging along the lower lip to form an *F*:

For

A

He stopped.

"For a what?" Madame Xanadu asked.

In his memory, Johnny Quick now snapped forward, his face a blur again, moving so fast, even here in Barry's memory, moving so fast . . .

He reached out and wrestled the memory under his control again, scrolling it back, watching.

Three ex to the quantity . . .

. . . nine why zee . . .

for a . . .

And nothing.

Nothing came next. Except for a speeded-up Johnny Quick snarling in rage and triumph as he lunged at Barry, reaching out with those hands that even the Flash could not evade, pummeling . . .

Barry snapped open his eyes as Johnny Quick's first impossibly fast blow landed. The memory of the punch forced a grunt out of him even as he came out of the hypnotic trance, feeling groggy and not quite himself. Jerking in his seat, he teetered precariously, then toppled over, crashing down with the chair.

Madame Xanadu came around the table, her expression one of shocked concern. "Are you all right?"

He lay there for a moment, not pondering the answer, but rather wondering if he would ever truly be all right again. Shrugging off her question and declining her extended hand, he gathered himself to his feet, righted the chair, and sat down again. He was still foggy from the hypnosis and it was hard to concentrate.

"I don't get it," he murmured. "It doesn't make any sense."

Retaking her seat, Madame Xanadu also regained her composure. "Are you certain you heard it all?"

"Yes."

And it was nonsense.

Absolute nonsense.

Three ex to the quantity nine why zee for a . . "For a *what?* What does it mean?" Barry slammed his fist on the table. "Is the rest of it in his head? Is he—"

"Slow down," Madame Xanadu said.

Seething, Barry glared at her. Just behind his lips, the words surged, ready to come out. *Slow down? Are you nuts? It's not time to slow down! It's time to speed up!*

But he thought of Hocus Pocus and the baseball stadium and the House of Mirrors back on Earth 1. Slowing down had saved him.

She was right.

"A mantra need not be a logical construct," she told him. "It serves to focus the mind, just as my ring and my voice focused yours."

"Are you saying Johnny Quick is hypnotizing himself in order to access the Speed Force?"

She thought for a moment. "I'm saying that the purpose of a thing may be in its mere existence, not necessarily in its details."

Barry drew in a deep breath and held it long enough that he felt a tightness in his chest. Then he exhaled slowly, feeling the stress and the tension and the confusion leave him.

He was smart. As smart as any other version of Barry Allen. He could figure this out.

"Three ex to the quantity nine why zee for a . . ." he mumbled. Something about it wasn't right. He said it again.

It was that "the quantity" bit that bothered him. And the *zee*, for that matter. They didn't seem to fit. Everything except for *zee* was a real word, and everything except for *quantity* was a single syllable.

Those two just didn't seem to fit.

What if . . . What if they did, though?

What if *zee* wasn't supposed to be a word? What if it was the letter Z?

Along those lines . . . Yes. Yes. He was shaking off the effects of the hypnotic state, and things were coming together much more quickly now. What if he'd made some very simple errors? Like switching out homophones: Maybe it wasn't *to*, but *two*. Maybe it wasn't *ex*, but X.

And about *quantity* . . . A quantity was an amount of something, yes, but it was also a mathematical term that referred to grouping numbers and variables together in parentheses. Once you removed the words "the quantity" from what he'd heard, everything else could be interpreted as a letter or a number.

It wasn't a sentence or a phrase. It was a *formula*. Or, more accurately, an *expression*, since it didn't equal anything.

As a mathematical expression, it would look like this:

3X2(9YZ)4A

He rattled it off again, this time not letting it droop at the end as though deprived of air. This time, he said it with full force and confidence, knowing it was complete unto itself.

Madame Xanadu watched him closely as it spilled out of him.

"3X2(9YZ)4A."

Nothing. This was pointless.

"Try again," she whispered, as though sensing his skepticism.

"3X2(9YZ)4A."

Still nothing. His patience wore thin.

"You're almost there," she said.

"3X2(9YZ)4A," he said. "3X2(9YZ)4A," he said again.

He felt something. Almost a . . . tug. Some kind of pull at the very outer, wispy reaches of his consciousness.

So he said it again. And again. And again. He said it faster and faster. The tug became stronger. He spoke the formula over and over, uttering it hundreds of times in the space of a single second, his lips and tongue blurring with speed, his voice unbearable to human ears, so fast and high-pitched it became.

The windows in Madame Xanadu's shop shivered. Her collection of mason jars vibrated at his inaudible voice.

"3X2(9YZ)4A." Over and over, and the tug became powerful, potent. Electricity crackled around him.

This is what he did. He focused on it and he practiced it over and over again. And just like someone who gets hypnotized

often can go under more easily each time, he got better at it. All
he has to do is say it once and he's "in" again.

Madame Xanadu pulled back and shielded her eyes with
her hands as lightning spat and zapped around Barry in a
coruscating halo of yellow and red. He stood up. The world
had gone perfectly still, stuck between the ticks of a stop-
watch. Even the air was frozen in place.

Barry was moving faster than he'd ever moved before,
and he was just standing there. His body hummed with the
Speed Force, channeled along a pure, unobstructed connection. It was like the difference between a dammed-up river
and one flowing free. He thought he'd known speed before.

Now he knew speed.

"I can beat him," Barry said, and the words were out of
his mouth in an imperceptible picosecond.

"I can beat him," he said again, slowing down. The world
and its motion, its sound, its life, spun up around him, like
an old record on a turntable that's just been plugged in.

Madame Xanadu smiled. "Indeed. I think you're ready,"
she said.

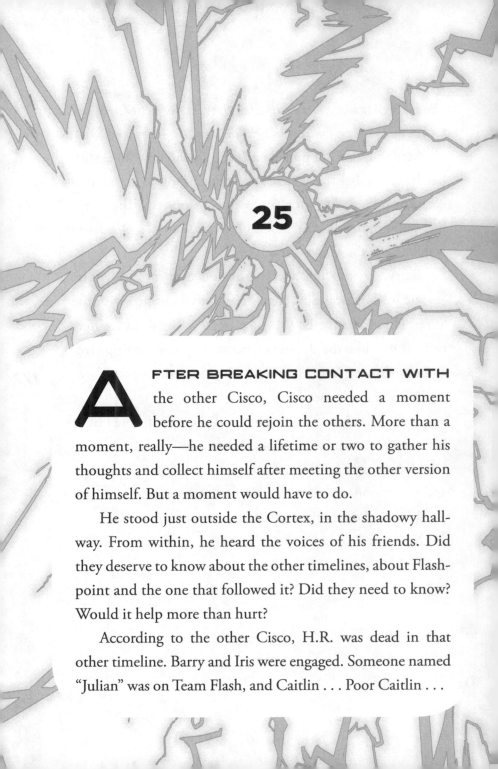

25

AFTER BREAKING CONTACT WITH the other Cisco, Cisco needed a moment before he could rejoin the others. More than a moment, really—he needed a lifetime or two to gather his thoughts and collect himself after meeting the other version of himself. But a moment would have to do.

He stood just outside the Cortex, in the shadowy hallway. From within, he heard the voices of his friends. Did they deserve to know about the other timelines, about Flashpoint and the one that followed it? Did they need to know? Would it help more than hurt?

According to the other Cisco, H.R. was dead in that other timeline. Barry and Iris were engaged. Someone named "Julian" was on Team Flash, and Caitlin . . . Poor Caitlin . . .

He shuddered. He didn't want to think about it.

What to tell them? What to tell them? The question tormented him. Alternate Earths were one thing, but this . . . This was different. This was *them*. Actual versions of themselves, just living out different lives because of a choice Barry had or had not made.

Could he tell H.R. he'd been killed by some creature called *Savitar*? Would it help or hurt Barry and Iris's relationship to tell them they were engaged? And how would Caitlin feel, knowing she had become Killer Frost and nearly killed everyone on Team Flash?

He suddenly felt as though he had become his own reflection in a pond, one stirred by a thrown stone. He was rippling, becoming unreal and indistinct. He had to fight to remain in the world. He knew this wasn't ACTUALLY happening. It was all in his head, the side effect of learning that maybe he was just a version of himself, not the real deal. What would that do to the others?

No. He couldn't tell them, he decided. He wouldn't. For all he knew, it was all still a ruse. He was 99.99999 percent certain that the other Cisco was exactly who and what he claimed to be, but in a world with telepathic gorillas, techno-magicians, and the occasional time-traveling psychopath, it was best to keep his options open.

He would say nothing. Not until he could talk to Barry and ask him about that night at Joe's house, the night after they'd defeated Zoom.

For now, he would just . . . pretend.

He cleared his throat, ran his hands through his hair, and plastered a grin on his face as he rounded the corner and strode into the Cortex and joined his friends.

After class was over, Wally sped back to S.T.A.R. Labs. Iris met him in the Cortex and walked with him to Cisco's workshop, where Cisco was putting the finishing touches on what looked like a standard scuba-diving wet suit.

"Ah, but it is *not* a standard scuba suit!" Cisco crowed, lifting it so that it unfurled like a flag before him. Flat black, it gleamed as if already wet, though it was dry. Slight ridges ran over its shoulders and met in the center of the chest at a raised circle. "I incorporated most of the same electronics that are in the Kid Flash costume, including comms so we can talk. And now the pièce de résistance . . ." With a flourish, Cisco twisted a Flash logo into the raised circle. It clicked into place. "Now you're set."

"'*Most* of the same electronics'?" Wally raised an eyebrow as he took the suit.

"I didn't have all day. I did the best I could."

Wally did a happy little dance. "I get to Kid Flash

around underground!" He held up both hands to forestall Iris's objections. Just the look on her face screamed *Worry!* "Don't worry. I'll be careful *and* effective."

"All I was going to say," Iris told him, "is take H.R. with you."

Wally laughed. "Oh, wait. You're serious."

"Everyone needs backup. No matter who you are or how fast you can run. If you're underground, you need someone above, and he's the only one available right now. I need to stay here for now. So, you take H.R. Got it?"

Wally nodded slowly. "Got it."

"Begone!" Cisco commanded. "Flash about and figure out the deal with Earthworm."

"Aye-aye, Cap'n!" Wally saluted.

After a moment, Cisco saluted back. "That was actually much cooler than I thought it would be," he admitted.

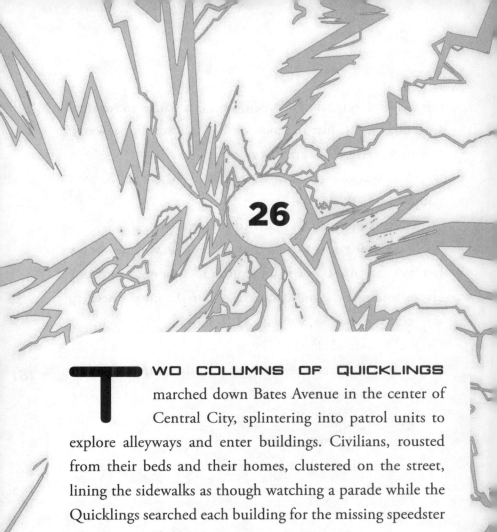

26

TWO COLUMNS OF QUICKLINGS
marched down Bates Avenue in the center of
Central City, splintering into patrol units to
explore alleyways and enter buildings. Civilians, rousted
from their beds and their homes, clustered on the street,
lining the sidewalks as though watching a parade while the
Quicklings searched each building for the missing speedster
who'd so vexed their master.

Barry watched them from a rooftop. Bates Avenue drew
a straight line from S.T.A.R. Labs to one of the blockaded
exits from town. The perfect place for an ambush.

So . . . he ambushed.

Racing down the side of the building, he spun his arms,
sending out whirlwinds at the Quicklings massed on the

street. They scattered in a panic and Barry waded into them, disarming each soldier of his or her weapon and stacking them up on the sidewalk. Then, while they were still in shock over the disappearance of their weapons, he just blasted through them, tripping a Quickling here, knocking one into another there, swinging one by the arm until he went stumbling off to crash into a clot of more Quicklings. In less than ten seconds, he'd taken out a squadron of close to fifty soldiers. They lay strewn on the street in befuddlement, groaning and gasping.

The crowd of civilians didn't know what to make of it. To them, the red-and-yellow burst of lightning that usually presaged some sort of horror show had just wiped out an entire group of their daily tormentors. No one knew whether to run for cover or cheer.

Barry tried to make it easy for them. He slowed down to human speed and stood in the center of the street, posing with one foot propped up on the chest of a fallen Quickling.

"Hey, there, Central City! There's a new speedster in town, and things are gonna change!"

A Quickling who'd managed to stand crept up behind Barry, who speedily spun around and knocked the man back down, but not before snatching his helmet right off his head. With a comically perplexed expression, the man crumpled to a heap on the ground.

Barry slipped the helmet on and triggered the built-in microphone that broadcast to a PA system mounted on one of the Quickling tanks. Usually, it was used to order crowds to disperse.

The Flash had a different use in mind.

"JOHNNY QUICK!" his voice boomed out, echoing down the alleys and streets of the city. "I KNOW WHO YOU REALLY ARE! I'M CALLING YOU OUT! COME OUT FROM BEHIND YOUR WALLS, YOU COWARD, AND FACE ME!"

Between the words *face* and *me*, a thundercrack exploded along Bates Avenue as something hurtling far beyond the speed of sound roared into place. Windows in a two-block radius shattered, raining glass down on the streets. Barry sped into action, knocking people out of the way of the sharp, glittering storm.

Speedsters could prevent the broken-glass syndrome inherent in going through the sound barrier by maintaining a subtle internal vibration. But clearly Johnny Quick just didn't care.

Quick skidded to a halt a few feet from Barry, his body rippling with electricity. Even through the vibrational blur of his face, Barry detected a haughty sneer.

"Think you know who I am?" Quick snapped. "I'm

more interested in who *you* are. Because you look *very* familiar, but you shouldn't."

"Ever look in a mirror?" Barry cracked gruffly.

"I don't know what you're talking about," Johnny Quick
snarled. "I watched Barry Allen die. Right in front of me. He
took the brunt of the lightning bolt that night, and it fried
him pretty damn good. How do you look just like him?"

Barry blinked. If that was true . . . then who *was* Johnny
Quick? Maybe Quick was just lying. Or maybe Barry Allen
had been driven insane that night and *thought* he was someone else, someone named Johnny Quick . . .

"Want this back?" Quick taunted, holding up Barry's
cowl. "Catch."

He tossed it into the air between them—but before Barry
could react, Johnny Quick was already running toward him.

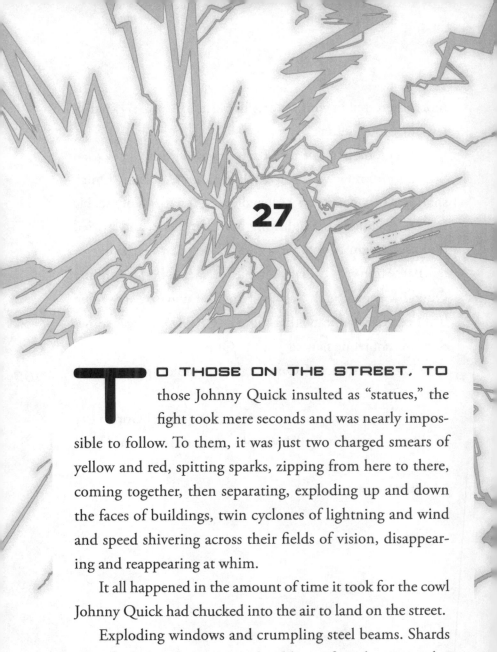

27

TO THOSE ON THE STREET, TO those Johnny Quick insulted as "statues," the fight took mere seconds and was nearly impossible to follow. To them, it was just two charged smears of yellow and red, spitting sparks, zipping from here to there, coming together, then separating, exploding up and down the faces of buildings, twin cyclones of lightning and wind and speed shivering across their fields of vision, disappearing and reappearing at whim.

It all happened in the amount of time it took for the cowl Johnny Quick had chucked into the air to land on the street.

Exploding windows and crumpling steel beams. Shards of melted glass frozen in midair like perfect abstract sculptures formed by the hands of invisible gods.

There was scarcely enough time to think, scarcely enough time to choose sides. But each denizen of Central City, somewhere in the fast-thinking, reflex-generating cul-de-sac of his or her brain, made that decision, chose that side, before the fight even began. For four years, they'd lived under the yoke and the terror of Johnny Quick. Anything had to be better than that, right?

Right?

The newcomer . . . he had to be *better*.

There was no time to pick a warrior and cheer him to victory, but they did it anyway; before the battle ended, the people of Central City made their choice and within the confines of their own thoughts screamed out for the newcomer to emerge victorious.

And when it was over, peals of smoke unfurled where feet friction-burned the street macadam, tar ran like water in footprint-shaped puddles, and one victor stood tall and triumphant. That's what it looked like to the mere mortals on the street that day.

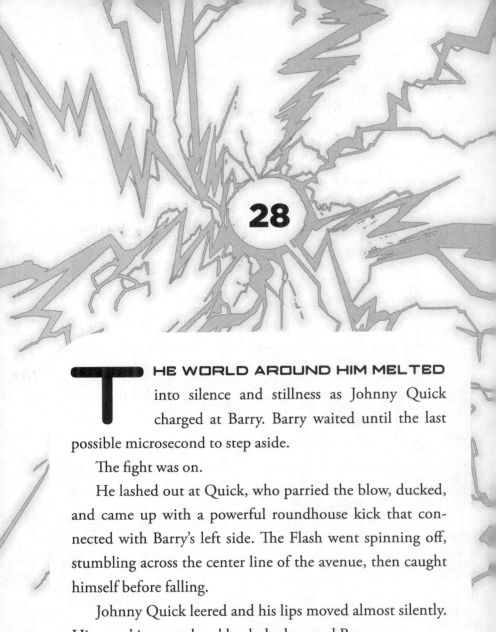

28

THE WORLD AROUND HIM MELTED into silence and stillness as Johnny Quick charged at Barry. Barry waited until the last possible microsecond to step aside.

The fight was on.

He lashed out at Quick, who parried the blow, ducked, and came up with a powerful roundhouse kick that connected with Barry's left side. The Flash went spinning off, stumbling across the center line of the avenue, then caught himself before falling.

Johnny Quick leered and his lips moved almost silently. His speed increased and he dashed toward Barry.

Barry stood still for half a microsecond, letting Johnny think he was an easy target.

And then he whispered to himself, "3X2(9YZ)4A."

He couldn't read the expression on Johnny's blurred face, but the man's body language said it all. As Barry's speed took a leap up to a new rung on the ladder, Quick's whole body seemed to recoil in shock. Barry ran toward him, lashing out with a fist as he did so. He smashed right into Johnny's jaw, a brutal haymaker that knocked Quick back thirty feet in a haze of electricity and the blur of speed.

"You think you'll make a difference here?" Quick sneered. "Even if you beat me, you'll still have to deal with the others."

"Beating you will be enough for now," Barry said, lunging.

"Do you have any idea what I've been through these past four years?" Quick demanded, juking to one side. "I made this place my sanctuary, my haven from the rest of the Crime Syndicate, but it turned out to be a gilded cage. I'm the fastest man alive, and I'm stuck here!"

Quick dashed up the side of the nearest building. Barry followed him, charging up the wall with ease. "Are you really trying to play on my *sympathy*? You murdered eighty thousand people! And for what? What had they done to you?"

"Done to me? Nothing." Quick launched a savage kick that Barry only barely dodged. "I did it because it *worked*, you idiot. In thirty seconds, I made this town *mine.*

Super-efficient, right? What would *you* have done—gone around and tried to *persuade* everyone?"

Seething, Barry grabbed hold of Quick's wrist and spun him around. "I would have let them live their lives!"

"Free will?" Quick chortled, amused at the mere thought. "In the time it takes them to decide whether to yawn or not, we can tear up roads, build skyscrapers, eradicate landmarks . . . Free will is obsolete. It only belongs to those who actually have the time and the speed to exercise it. That's *us*."

Barry punched him so hard that Quick spun around and slipped up a wall, defying gravity. Barry ran up the wall after him, hoping to land another blow, but Quick managed to shake it off and dodge him.

They chased each other around the city that way, running up buildings, then down, then tearing across them, racing perpendicular to the pull of gravity, moving so fast that Newtonian physics couldn't keep up. They were quantum speedsters, their velocities unmatched by anything save perhaps the tachyons.

At the corner of Bates Avenue and Novick Street, Barry tackled Quick to the ground. The two of them skidded along the road for two blocks; melted tar washed up in their wake and resolidified, making the road look as though it had been somehow unzipped.

"You think you're a ruler, but you're just another scared bully!" Barry cried out. "Hurting others before they can hurt you!"

"Oh, you wound me," Quick said sarcastically. They were still skidding along in the drags between milliseconds. "I did what I had to do to protect myself. I would do it again. If you had any brains, you'd've signed on with me and—"

"Shut up!"

Barry struggled with Johnny, rolling on top of him, trying to pin him to the ground. Quick unleashed a flurry of punches. Barry was faster now, thanks to the speed mantra, but so many punches in such a short span of time . . . some of them landed. He tasted his own blood, felt a cut open on his left cheek.

He returned the blows, raining them down on Quick with a ferocity he did not know he possessed. Zoom had murdered Henry Allen. The Reverse-Flash had killed Nora Allen. But Quick's crimes, though less personal, seemed more extreme. Johnny Quick had casually killed thousands and then, for years, terrorized those who remained. All to guarantee his own safety and power. All to give himself a safe base of operations from which he could hurt more and more people until the entire world was open to him.

"No more!" Barry heard himself shouting. "No more!"

Johnny lurched under the force of the pummeling,

throwing Barry off of him. He staggered to his feet, breathing hard. Barry picked himself up and—ignoring a sharp pain in his rib cage—grappled with Johnny, spinning him around. Barry hit him once in the face, then twice, then a third time, his fist moving at invisible speed.

Johnny rallied, bringing up his hands, jabbing at Barry with a quick one-two.

Barry dodged left, then right, then lowered his head and plowed right into Johnny with his shoulder, driving the other man to the ground. Johnny flailed for a moment; Barry stepped on his chest.

"Stay. Down," he said through clenched teeth.

Johnny sputtered and struggled, then, exhaling loudly, gave up and collapsed, his eyes closing as he passed out.

The world rushed back in. Barry could hear the air again, the breathing of the crowd. He was surrounded by hundreds of Central City denizens, all of whom stared at him in disbelief.

"He won't hurt you anymore," Barry told them, heaving his breath. "I promise."

They didn't seem to believe him. He couldn't blame them. Years of oppression at the hands of one speedster wouldn't just evaporate on the say-so of another.

He crouched down next to the unconscious Johnny Quick. Quick had claimed to have watched Barry Allen die, so he couldn't *be* Barry Allen, right? And now that he could study the man, Barry had his doubts. Johnny Quick had a different build—less of a runner, more of a wrestler or a boxer.

For the first time, Quick's face wasn't blurred. Barry gulped. He looked familiar . . .

Peeling back the cowl, he froze in shock as a thatch of blond hair came into view.

Familiar. Yes. Very. Barry knew this man. Or, rather, *had* known him.

It was Eddie. Eddie Thawne!

Sheer chance, Johnny Quick had told him. *I was in the lab at CCPD the night the particle accelerator blew.*

Eddie was a detective. He had probably come to the lab to visit Earth 27's Barry Allen for information. The lightning bolt had killed Barry and made Eddie a speedster.

Just as the Rogues were good here, Eddie—a conscientious cop on Earth 1, a man who had willingly sacrificed his life for the greater good—was corrupt and evil here. He'd probably been a dirty cop, like this Earth's version of Fred Chyre.

He wondered briefly about the graves he'd seen, for Cisco and the others, and if they had been bad guys on Earth 27. Had the Earth 27 Barry Allen been evil, too?

He would never know. And, he realized in that moment, he didn't *need* to know.

What he needed was simple: Hocus Pocus's wand and a way back home.

Barry retrieved his cowl from where Eddie had tossed it and sighed. Maybe not so simple after all.

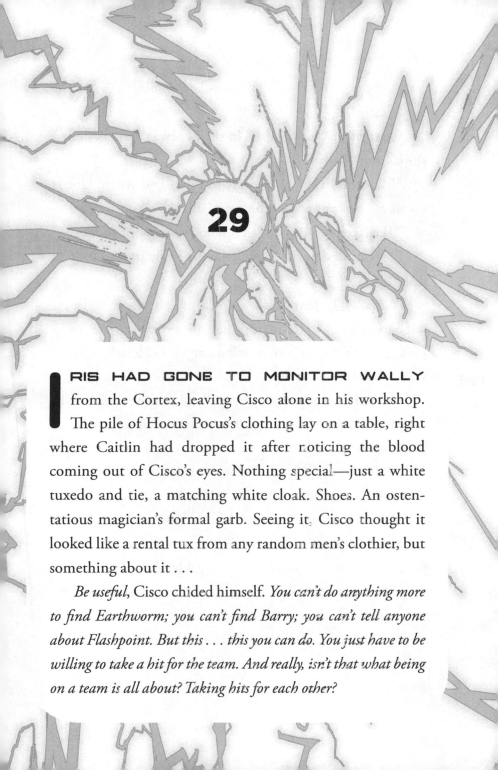

29

IRIS HAD GONE TO MONITOR WALLY from the Cortex, leaving Cisco alone in his workshop. The pile of Hocus Pocus's clothing lay on a table, right where Caitlin had dropped it after noticing the blood coming out of Cisco's eyes. Nothing special—just a white tuxedo and tie, a matching white cloak. Shoes. An ostentatious magician's formal garb. Seeing it, Cisco thought it looked like a rental tux from any random men's clothier, but something about it . . .

Be useful, Cisco chided himself. *You can't do anything more to find Earthworm; you can't find Barry; you can't tell anyone about Flashpoint. But this . . . this you can do. You just have to be willing to take a hit for the team. And really, isn't that what being on a team is all about? Taking hits for each other?*

"Cisco?"

He turned. Caitlin stood in the doorway. "Don't do it," she cautioned.

"I have to. It's the only way to figure out where Hocus Pocus comes from, where he went."

"The last time you tried this, blood shot out of your eyes."

He chuckled mirthlessly. "It didn't really shoot. It kinda dribbled."

"Cisco!" She stomped over to him and interposed herself between him and the clothing. "Parse sentences and nit-pick all you want, but you can't do any good for the team if you kill yourself!"

"Then help me *not* kill myself," he told her, leaning in urgently. "Figure out a way to let me vibe his gear without bleeding out."

Caitlin stared at him, not backing down, but then relented. "Look, haemolacria isn't very well understood."

"I don't even understand the word," he cracked.

She finally smiled at him. "Haemolacria. From the Latin for . . . Oh, never mind. It's crying blood, OK? It's really rare. Not that many cases at all in the world, and for some reason, most of them are in Tennessee."

"Now I know you're just messing with me."

"Nope. Anyway, let me do a little research. In the meantime, don't go *near* that." She pointed at the pile of clothes.

Cisco raised his hand. "Scout's honor."

"I know you weren't a Boy Scout, but I choose to trust you anyway," she said with a smirk.

Jittery and agitated, H.R. paced the length of the hallway as Kid Flash struggled into the wet suit. "I just think there's a better way to do this," he complained. "Better than sending you down there where it's dark and creepy and wet and stinky and decidedly decaf, if you get my drift. Couldn't we use a drone?"

Wally shrugged. "Too many random protrusions and pipes down there. Plus, the signal for a drone *might* get through all the metal and concrete, but there'd be significant lag."

"Meaning . . ."

"Meaning by the time you could react to something, a drone would have crashed into it already."

"Crash-ola," H.R. whispered, and mimed an explosion, splaying out his fingers.

"Crash-a-roo," Wally agreed. "Don't worry. I'll be fine. I've got speed, remember?"

"Just be—"

"Careful. I know." Wally blew out a breath in exasperation. "Man! It's like I've never been careful before! Do I have a rep or something?"

"Well, you used to street-race. Which I'm told is a pretty dangerous pastime."

"And you gulp down toxic amounts of coffee on the regular. So . . . pot, meet kettle."

H.R. recoiled in bafflement and offense. "First of all, young sir, it is impossible to partake of an excess of what I lovingly and affectionately refer to simply as . . . *the Bean*. Second of all, I don't understand the second bit about pots and kettles, nor do I see the relevance of kitchen apparatus."

Wally laughed. "Haven't you ever heard the expression *That's like the pot calling the kettle black*?"

"Well, that's a ridiculous thing to say. Is that a thing on this Earth? My kettle is a lovely blue and my pots are stainless steel. Why in the world would—"

"Bored now," Wally said. He saluted H.R. and took off for the museum.

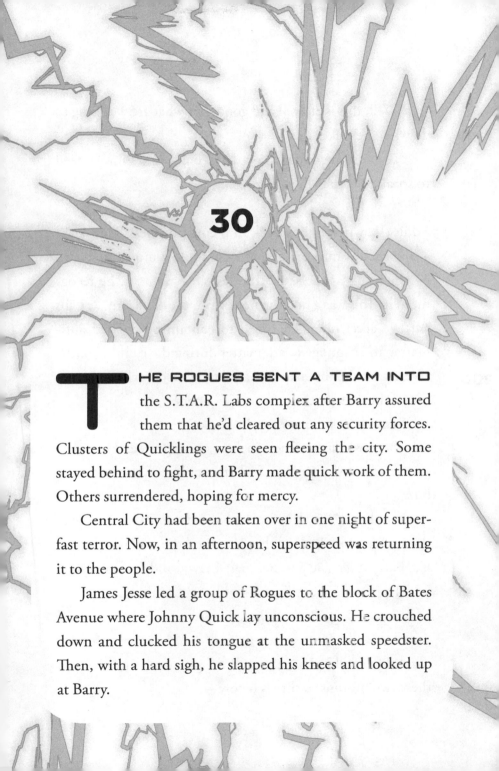

30

THE ROGUES SENT A TEAM INTO
the S.T.A.R. Labs complex after Barry assured
them that he'd cleared out any security forces.
Clusters of Quicklings were seen fleeing the city. Some
stayed behind to fight, and Barry made quick work of them.
Others surrendered, hoping for mercy.

Central City had been taken over in one night of superfast terror. Now, in an afternoon, superspeed was returning
it to the people.

James Jesse led a group of Rogues to the block of Bates
Avenue where Johnny Quick lay unconscious. He crouched
down and clucked his tongue at the unmasked speedster.
Then, with a hard sigh, he slapped his knees and looked up
at Barry.

"Well, this is all well and good, but what are we going to do when he wakes up?"

"I have some thoughts on that," Barry told him. "I need to speak to your tech expert."

Eddie Thawne blinked back into consciousness. He was in a tiny room, small enough that he could almost touch two parallel walls at the same time. After a moment, he recognized it: This was a holding node from the old S.T.A.R. Labs particle accelerator. Designed to contain off-spewed antimatter and expunged dark matter during the running of the accelerator, it was made of a metallic alloy called promethium, blended with advanced polymers.

Someone had jury-rigged a bunk.

There was a fly stuck in here, it appeared. He cast a glance around, trying to find the source of the annoying buzzing.

Just then, the wall before him slid up, revealing a pane of thick, clear glass. Beyond the glass stood the man who looked like Barry Allen and another man Thawne didn't recognize.

"Hi, there!" the Allen look-alike said, smiling.

Keep smiling, Thawne thought. *It makes it easier to knock your teeth out.* He reached toward the glass, vibrating his hand. He would phase through the glass wall and then rip these two morons to shreds before—

His hand *thunk*ed against the glass. It had stopped vibrating of its own accord.

Setting his jaw, Thawne once again started vibrating his hand and reached out to the—

It happened again! His hand touched the glass instead of going through it. And that blasted fly was still buzzing around, driving him nuts.

"What did you do to me?" he shouted, now pressing his body up against the glass. "What did you do?"

"Barry Allen" gestured to the other man. "Meet Hartley Rathaway. Sonics genius."

"Hear a fly buzzing around in there?" Rathaway asked with a confident smirk. "That's not a fly at all. It's aural residue from an ultrasonic frequency I developed. You can't hear most of it, but the stuff too high for you to lock in on gets into your brain and rattles you just enough to keep you from focusing on your speed or your mantra."

Eddie gnashed his teeth and stepped back into the center of his cell. "Bull! 3X2(9YZ)4A." He looked down at his hands. They vibrated, but slowly. So slowly.

"3X2(9YZ)4A!" he cried again.

HyperHeaven loomed just beyond his grasp. He couldn't feel its tendrils of power around him. Every time he thought he'd grasped it, it flowed through his fingers like mercury. He felt as though he were moving through wet cement.

"3X2(9YZ)4A!"

Nothing. His hand was less a vibrating instrument of swift lethality and more a palsied claw. He could summon the edges of his speed, but not use it.

He was a statue. They'd made him a damn statue.

"One question," the man who looked like Barry Allen said. "What were you doing in the lab that night?"

"What do you *think* I was doing there?" Thawne snarled. "I was destroying *evidence*, you moron. And I got to watch that pencil-neck loser who looks like you get fried by lightning in the bargain."

The Allen look-alike nodded sadly and gestured to Rathaway, who pushed a button. The wall began to slide down between them again.

"I'll get out of here!" Thawne yelled. "I'll find a way!" He pounded with both fists on the glass, which didn't budge. "I'll get out of here and kill you all!"

"I'm sure you will, Eddie," said the man who looked like Barry Allen, and the wall slid shut.

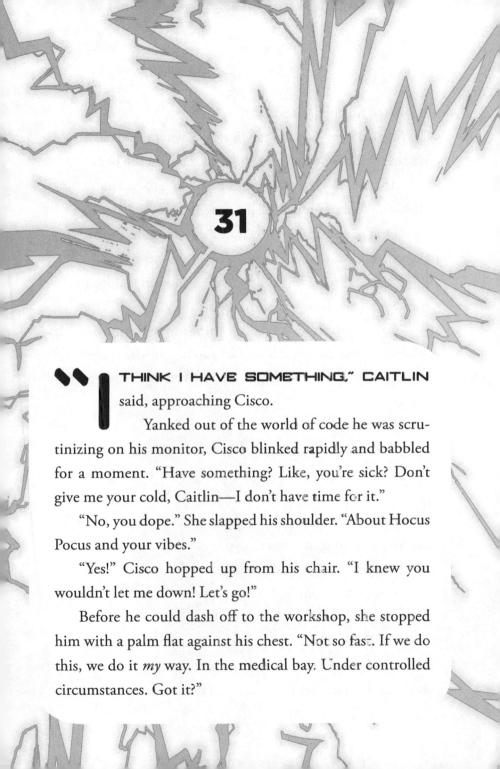

31

"I THINK I HAVE SOMETHING," CAITLIN said, approaching Cisco.

Yanked out of the world of code he was scrutinizing on his monitor, Cisco blinked rapidly and babbled for a moment. "Have something? Like, you're sick? Don't give me your cold, Caitlin—I don't have time for it."

"No, you dope." She slapped his shoulder. "About Hocus Pocus and your vibes."

"Yes!" Cisco hopped up from his chair. "I knew you wouldn't let me down! Let's go!"

Before he could dash off to the workshop, she stopped him with a palm flat against his chest. "Not so fast. If we do this, we do it *my* way. In the medical bay. Under controlled circumstances. Got it?"

Cisco fidgeted. "Yeah, OK . . ."

She led him into the medical bay, where she had an IV waiting. Hocus Pocus's clothing was piled on the bed.

"Another IV?" he whined. "I'm starting to feel like a pincushion. You're gonna be calling me Porcupine Pete."

"Don't be a baby. Sit down." She gestured to the bed, on the side opposite where she'd dumped the clothing.

Cisco relented and sat down, then allowed Caitlin to jab him with a needle in order to insert the IV.

"So," Caitlin said as she set things up, "haemolacria is usually caused by something like tumors, or damage to the conjunctiva or tears in the tear ducts. You don't have any of those."

"For which I'm grateful, by the way."

"But," she went on, twisting the dial on the IV so that the solution began to drip, "there is some research to indicate that stress can cause bloody tears. My theory is that whatever you're vibing, it's so intense and stressful that it's causing a bleed somewhere in your ocular system."

Thinking of the rapid-fire images, of the sickly green pall to the vibe, the man in black, Cisco nodded. "Yeah, it was pretty intense."

"So, I'm hooking you up to an intravenous solution of beta-blockers and antianxiety meds. To keep you on an even keel." She pursed her lips and tilted her head back and forth

SANTA MONICA PUBLIC
LIBRARY

Items that you checked out

Title: Johnny Quick
Due: Saturday, September 14, 2019

Total items: 1
Account balance: $1.20
8/17/2019 11:14 AM
Checked out: 3
Overdue: 0
Hold requests: 0
Ready for pickup: 0

Thank you for visiting the Santa Monica Public
Library.

the way she did when she had bad news to deliver. "Uh, there's a chance you'll pass out."

Cisco shrugged. "Isn't there always?"

"You ready?"

"I feel pretty loose, if that's what you mean." It was true. He was the chillest he'd ever been in his life.

"The meds are taking hold. OK, then . . ." After a moment's hesitation, she picked up Hocus Pocus's clothes and dropped them into Cisco's lap.

And Cisco . . .

Vibed.

This time, it all made sense. Everything was still herky-jerky and out of focus, but he was able to process it, to slow it down in his mind.

The man in black . . . That was Abra Kadabra. And what Cisco was seeing—the chase through S.T.A.R. Labs, Joe wielding the gun—he realized now that these images were from the other timeline, the one the other Cisco called home. The world after "Flashpoint."

Was there a connection somehow? Between Abra Kadabra and Flashpoint and Hocus Pocus and the world Cisco lived in?

He pushed further. And he understood. At last, he understood, and it all made perfect sense.

The clothing tumbled out of his nerveless fingers and fell to the floor. He felt warm and safe and more relaxed than ever before in his life.

"I get it," he told Caitlin, his voice thick and dream-like in his own ears. "I know where Hocus Pocus is."

"Great!" Caitlin exclaimed.

And Cisco quite peacefully and happily passed out.

The service node near the museum was the scene of the latest body dump, so it made sense to start there, on the theory that the clues would be fresher. According to Cisco and Iris's makeshift map overlay, there had been two other bodies found in proximity to that node over the past year, as well. Wally was hoping to find something worthwhile.

Hoping was probably too mild a term. He was eager.

Actually, on second thought . . . *eager* was too mild, too. He was *fervent*. Zealous.

Zealous. He liked the sound of that, turning it over in his head as the wind whipped past him at Mach 2. Breaking the sound barrier usually meant shattering any nearby glass, but Barry had delved into his treasure trove of science tidbits—Flash Facts—and revealed that if a speedster maintained a certain internal vibration, he could break the sound barrier without also breaking every window in a three-block radius.

Zealous. It sounded sleek and cool. It sounded aerodynamic. He liked that.

Zealous Kid Flash, reporting for duty, he thought as he neared the alleyway. He'd left H.R. racing to catch up to him. Whatever. Yeah, backup made sense, but the guy from Earth 19 was—no offense—not much of a fighter.

With a burst of static, Iris said in his ear, "Once you get down the ladder, you turn—"

"I know, I know. I remember the map." He shook his head to clear it. Cisco's rush-job wet suit had some bugs to work out. The static was really bothering him.

"Don't let anyone—"

"See me. Right. Got it." Ugh. That static!

"I'm in," he said. His voice came trickling back to him on a wave of feedback.

"Great!" Iris said. "Cisco didn't have time to install video cameras, so you'll have to narrate what you're seeing."

"I see a lot of dark. Hang on." He let go of the ladder with one hand and switched on the lamp Cisco had installed in the suit's headpiece. A grimy, slimy concrete wall leaped into view between the rungs of the ladder. "Oh, gross."

"What?" Iris demanded on a burst of static.

"I'm in a sewer," Wally deadpanned. "Use your imagination."

"Yuck." More static.

Wally batted at his ear, hoping to fix the speaker through sheer annoyance. No such luck.

He scrabbled down the ladder and stepped into a flow of sewage. The smell down here was pretty bad, worse than before. He slipped on the breathing mask Cisco had given him. Ah.

He turned left and made his way through the tunnel toward the service node near the museum. The splash of his feet formed a percussion to the vibrating crackle of ever-present static. Iris's voice would occasionally break through the static to ask a question, which Wally answered as best he could. He was trying to focus on looking for clues, and the distractions weren't helping.

Finally, he gave up. "Oh, hey, Iris, you're breaking up. Must be all the metal and concrete down here."

Before Iris could reply, Wally yanked the earpiece out and tossed it in the water. Good riddance.

Up ahead, he spied a cross tunnel. It was so narrow and low that he had to crawl through this one, using his elbows to pull himself along through the trickle of water and filth that dribbled along. He was beyond grateful for the wet suit, which kept him dry . . . except for the sweat that began to collect under it as he heaved himself through the tunnel.

As in the other part of the sewer, this tunnel opened out into a largish chamber clad in concrete, festooned with conduits and pipes. He waded through ankle-deep water the color of dryer lint until he came upon—as before—a U-bolt set into the wall. No scratchitti this time. But something else.

Blood.

He was sure of it. Right there on the wall, next to the U-bolt. A spray of it, maybe six inches long at its most extreme point. Wally gulped and took out his phone. As he'd been told, he put a quarter next to the stain for perspective, then started snapping pictures. For sure, this was where the latest victim, Herb Shawn, had met his end.

Crouched down to take the photos, his back started to ache. He stood to stretch and heard something behind him. Spinning around, he saw nothing.

Settle down, West. You're a speedster. Settle. Down.

Another sound. Somewhere out there in the dark. He looked around, then looked up. Something yellow and black flashed above him, leaping from the wall behind him to a spot just outside the range of his headlamp. He almost lost his grip on his phone, fumbled it, recovered it, and pointed it into the darkness with the camera on.

"Come out where I can see you!" he yelled.

For response, the thing out there hissed and leaped again, this time jumping up to the ceiling . . .

. . . and clinging there.

Wally craned his neck and looked up. His lamp pinned the thing there for a moment, but a moment was all it took. He was looking at a human form, one elongated at the limbs and torso so that it appeared too long and too thin to be a person. Its skin was yellow, its clothing black. It hissed at him again as he snapped pictures, his jaw hanging open at what his eyes presented to him.

Then the phone was knocked from his hands. The person—the thing—the person up above had thrown something and it knocked Wally's phone away as he held it up over his head . . .

. . . and kept going, smashing into his headlamp. The room was now lit only by a weak, flickering emergency light, which strobed a sickly yellow at irregular intervals. Just as his eyes adjusted, something smashed that, too, and plunged him instantly into darkness.

The darkest darkness Wally had ever known. There was absolutely no light of any kind, and he knew that the nearest light was fifteen feet straight up, without a ladder in sight. Or within his grasp.

"Not so brave now," came a voice from the dark. It wasn't above him. It was in front of him. Wally backed up, blind, feeling for the wall behind him. *Keep the wall to your back. Then at least you know he can't come up behind you.*

"Not so brave," the voice repeated, this time speaking

almost directly into his right ear. Wally shrieked and juked to his left, only to collide with a wall. He'd gotten turned around somehow. He didn't know how he was positioned in the room.

"Upworlders, so brave," the voice mocked, now coming from above. "So brave until their toys break and they see the real world."

Behind him now. Wally vibrated his hand and swung around, lashing out, catching only empty air.

A faint laugh echoed in the chamber.

"Upworlders think they're better. Stronger. With their toys and their light. No stink on them." The voice shifted again, now directly in front of him. "But it *all* stinks down here, Upworlder."

Wally threw a superspeed punch at the voice but missed again. The dark was all-encompassing, oppressive. It lay around and over him like a stifling, humid blanket.

"Do you know where I am? Do you?"

He thought the voice was coming from above, but couldn't be sure. A chittering sound reached him; the water around his feet churned, and he leaped back as tiny teeth sank into his ankle.

Cisco's wet suit was strong enough that it didn't break, but the teeth were sharp and strong; the bite stung even through the layers of the wet suit. Wally yelped and jumped back reflexively, slipping on his good foot and falling into the water. A jolt of pain ran from his tailbone to his shoulder blades.

He shook his leg. The thing biting him—it was a rat, he was sure—didn't let go, sinking its teeth in farther. He tried vibrating, and that did the trick—the rat squealed and squeaked in outrage as it disengaged. The sound of splashing reached him as the rat scampered away.

Whew.

"Upworlder, Upworlder . . ." the voice taunted.

"You're not going to keep killing people!" Wally said. "Not while I'm here!"

"How will you stop me when you can't see me?"

Wally lashed out with both hands, vibrating them just enough to cause wicked friction burns to whatever or whomever he struck. Up, down, left, right, ahead, behind—he was a whirlwind in human form.

After a few moments of that, he paused, holding his breath, listening.

Nothing.

Nothing.

He'd nailed Earthworm. Or scared him off. Or—

"All that speed," came the voice, and it was *right next to him.* "All that speed, so useless in the dark. You can't even run away . . ."

A finger touched his cheek, drew a line down to his jaw. Wally bit back a scream, turned to grab Earthworm, but all that was there was empty air, darkness, and the echo of a laugh.

And then the sound of water moving. Tiny splashes.

Tiny feet striking the water. Not a rat. Not this time.

No, not *a* rat.

Dozens of them. Maybe hundreds.

Racing toward him in the impenetrable dark . . .

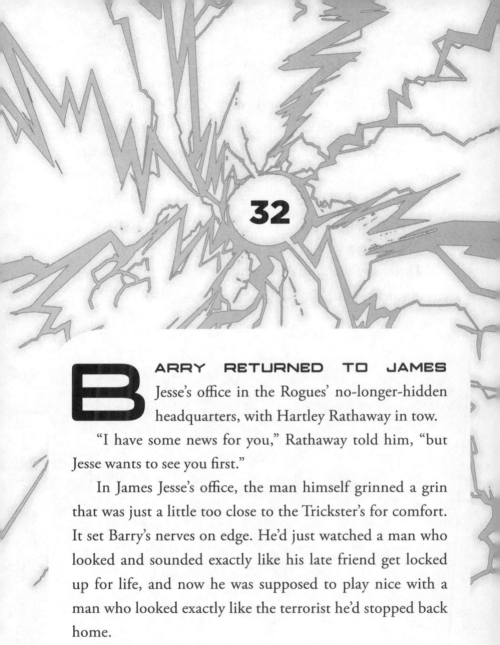

32

BARRY RETURNED TO JAMES Jesse's office in the Rogues' no-longer-hidden headquarters, with Hartley Rathaway in tow.

"I have some news for you," Rathaway told him, "but Jesse wants to see you first."

In James Jesse's office, the man himself grinned a grin that was just a little too close to the Trickster's for comfort. It set Barry's nerves on edge. He'd just watched a man who looked and sounded exactly like his late friend get locked up for life, and now he was supposed to play nice with a man who looked exactly like the terrorist he'd stopped back home.

What a world. *Worlds, really,* he amended.

"I promised you that if you helped us with Johnny

Quick, I'd help you find your missing property, didn't I?" James asked.

"Yes, but I know how difficult it . . ." Barry trailed off as James opened his desk drawer and withdrew something. He held it out to Barry.

It was Hocus Pocus's wand.

"Some of our scavengers found it and brought it in right before you arrived. We thought it was some of Quick's tech. Sorry I held out on you."

Taking the wand, Barry turned it over in his hands. "You had it all along." Maybe there was a little something of the Trickster in this James Jesse after all.

"More good news," Hartley said, holding up the wrecked tachyon harness. "This gizmo of yours makes no sense to me. But I think I can fix it. All of the components are in there, and it's obvious what's broken. I'm just repairing things. Connecting A to B. I don't have to understand why they need to connect. It's just obvious that they're supposed to."

"I appreciate that," Barry told him, with more calm than he'd thought to be possible. After defeating Johnny Quick, he'd felt a rush of triumph, followed by a seeping cold panic. Sure, he'd defeated the bad guy and saved the city, but he was still trapped in an alternate universe with no way home. Until now.

"I'll get right to work," Hartley said. "And then you can go . . . wherever it is you go."

Barry sighed. He'd never explained the Multiverse, and right now it seemed like too much to pile on after defeating Eddie. The people of Earth 27 had enough on their hands without having to worry about parallel universes and dimensions beyond their own.

And maybe, just maybe, he thought, he could help them in their efforts. Even after leaving. Maybe he could—

"While we wait for Hartley to finish up, someone wants to talk to you," James said, interrupting his thoughts. He ushered Barry through a door.

They entered a stairwell and went up. At the very top, James opened an emergency door and gestured for Barry to step outside.

It was a cool, clear day when he exited to the roof. Standing a little ways away, a man in a sweatshirt and jeans had his back to Barry, his arms outstretched and his face tilted to the sky. As Barry neared him, he realized that this was Clyde Mardon.

Mardon seemed to sense him. He dropped his arms and turned to Barry. "Hey, man," he said, a lopsided grin on his face. It was so discordant from the Clyde Mardon of Earth 1, a thug and a killer, that Barry was struck dumb for a moment.

"Uh, hey."

"They said I have you to thank for getting me out of that bummer of a tank. Gracias, dude." He stuck out his hand.

Barry couldn't help it; he chuckled as he clasped Mardon's hand. Here, fine, upstanding lawmen like Fred Chyre and Eddie Thawne were the scum of this Earth, while low-life crooks like Clyde Mardon were chill hippie dudes. In the enormity of the Multiverse, it seemed just about anything was possible.

"You're welcome. What will you do now that you're free?"

Mardon shrugged. "Try to find my brother, I guess. And then go where the wind takes me, man. Gonna stick around here a little while, though. See if I can whip up some righteous weather to undo some of the damage I did." He grinned in delight. "And maybe it's time to let people know it's a brand-new day, eh?"

Before Barry could respond, Mardon took a few steps back. Once again, he held his arms out and looked up to the sun.

Droplets of water began to condense out of the moisture in the air as a light mist coalesced. At the same time, the clouds overhead parted, drifting away and exposing the full blast of the sun.

A moment later, Barry's face split into a delighted grin and he realized he was applauding. The light mist and the sunlight met, and soon there were rainbows—bright and bold and resplendent in their glow—arcing all over Central City. Reflected in the windows and glass of the skyscrapers, the rainbows seemed to envelop the city and weave through it at the same time. The colors were gorgeous and bright and everywhere.

"Good for you, Weather Wizard."

Barry whispered it, but Mardon heard him anyway. He cracked a grin.

"Weather Wizard, huh? I like that, brother. Maybe I'll keep it."

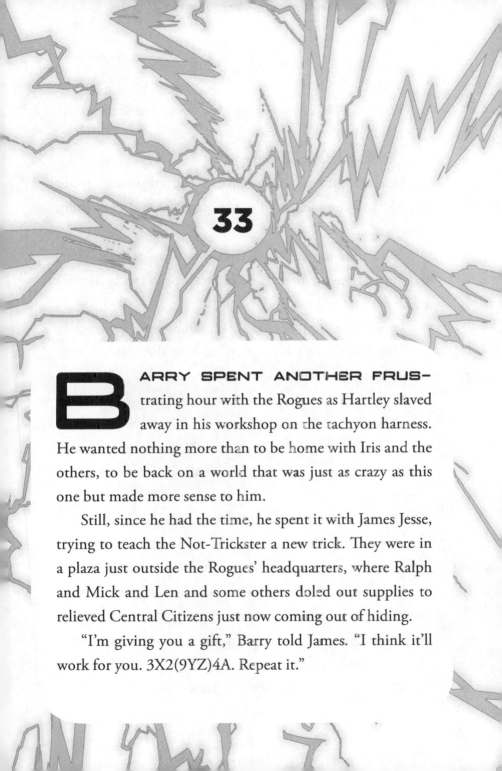

33

BARRY SPENT ANOTHER FRUS-trating hour with the Rogues as Hartley slaved away in his workshop on the tachyon harness. He wanted nothing more than to be home with Iris and the others, to be back on a world that was just as crazy as this one but made more sense to him.

Still, since he had the time, he spent it with James Jesse, trying to teach the Not-Trickster a new trick. They were in a plaza just outside the Rogues' headquarters, where Ralph and Mick and Len and some others doled out supplies to relieved Central Citizens just now coming out of hiding.

"I'm giving you a gift," Barry told James. "I think it'll work for you. 3X2(9YZ)4A. Repeat it."

With a blank look on his face, James replied, "3X2(9YZ)4A."

"Try it again. Feel anything?"

James said it again, slowly, then a third time, a bit more quickly and confidently. "I'm not sure," he said doubtfully. "Maybe."

"It'll come to you. Teach it to your people. Keep saying it. Concentrate on it. Eventually, you'll be as fast as he once was."

James's jaw dropped. "Are you kidding me?"

"Not even a little bit. I imagine even the Crime Syndicate of America will think twice about attacking a city protected by an army of superspeedsters. Central City will be the safest city on the planet."

Tears welled up in James's eyes. "I don't know how to thank you," he said, choking on a sob. "I don't even know how to start."

"Just take care of this city," Barry said. "And if you have the chance, spread the good, will you?"

James nodded, mute with gratitude and awe.

Barry noticed Len and Mick huddled together, gesturing wildly as they talked. "And if those guys get their hands on a freeze gun or a heat blaster, don't let them hold on to them. Just to be safe."

With a befuddled expression, James said, "Um, OK."

Hartley approached them with the harness slung over one shoulder. It had messy solder welts and a bulge of wiring at one end, but it looked whole.

"It's not pretty," Hartley apologized, "but I'm pretty sure it works."

"Pretty sure?"

Hartley shrugged. "No one's perfect."

"That's true." Barry slapped him on the shoulder. "Thanks for your help. Now I have to go."

The cowl didn't fit quite right, having been raggedly torn free from the rest of the costume. Barry tried a couple of different angles, but it kept slipping down to obscure his vision. He gave up and tucked it into his belt.

Usually he had to work up a decent head of steam before the tachyon harness kicked in. But with the exceptional speed granted to him by Eddie's formula, it would now be a piece of cake.

Barry crouched in a runner's pose, his fingertips on the pavement. A crowd had gathered to cheer him on and wish him farewell. Thanks to Clyde Mardon, it was a gorgeous day, warm enough to forgo a jacket, with just enough sunshine. He wondered what the weather was like back home, and smiled, knowing he would find out soon.

"3X2(9YZ)4A," he said under his breath, and felt the

Speed Force envelop him, a crepitating electricity that felt warm and safe and powerful.

He tapped the tachyon harness and took off at near-light speed, blasting through and out of Central City in less time than it took to blink.

The Multiverse opened before him, yawning wide. There was Kara and the rabbit in a cape and Jay Garrick and the boy screaming down lightning from the sky. And others, too, a blur of them, worlds beyond worlds, finite, but seeming to go on forever.

He caught a glimpse of the familiar skyline of Central City on Earth 2, its monorail glistening in the sun as it slid smoothly through the gaps between buildings.

He clutched Hocus Pocus's wand tightly in his hand as Earth 2 hovered in his sight.

No, not now. I'm going home.

He ran even faster. Earth 2 evaporated before his eyes, and Earth 1 loomed huge and impossible to miss before him.

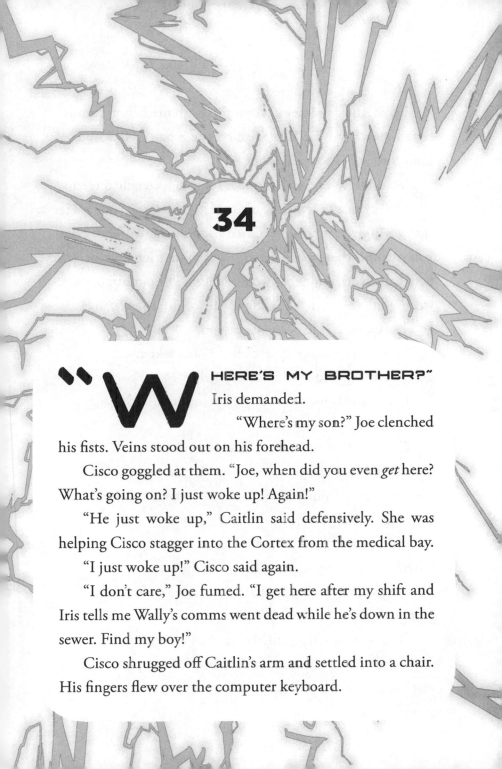

34

"WHERE'S MY BROTHER?"
Iris demanded.

"Where's my son?" Joe clenched his fists. Veins stood out on his forehead.

Cisco goggled at them. "Joe, when did you even *get* here? What's going on? I just woke up! Again!"

"He just woke up," Caitlin said defensively. She was helping Cisco stagger into the Cortex from the medical bay.

"I just woke up!" Cisco said again.

"I don't care," Joe fumed. "I get here after my shift and Iris tells me Wally's comms went dead while he's down in the sewer. Find my boy!"

Cisco shrugged off Caitlin's arm and settled into a chair. His fingers flew over the computer keyboard.

"Well, the good news is that the Flash medallion I trans-ferred over from the Kid Flash costume has a GPS tracker built into it," Cisco told them.

"And the bad news?" Joe asked through clenched teeth.

"So cynical!" H.R. exclaimed. "So untrusting." He threw a jolly arm around Cisco's shoulders. "Why would you assume there's bad news? My good friend Francisco here has a work ethic that would make a Puritan lumberjack weep. If he says there's a GPS in Wally's suit, then Wally is as good as located." He beamed at them.

"What are you doing back here?" Iris asked.

"Wally ditched me," H.R. replied.

Iris seethed. Joe rubbed his forehead. Could things get any worse?

Cisco's left eyelid twitched as screens lit up. "Well, uh, actually there *is* bad news. It seems that several feet of con-crete and metal pipes blocks the GPS signal. So, yeah, we can't locate Wally."

H.R. pursed his lips and nodded. He pulled away from Cisco. "You're on your own here, buddy."

Joe swore so violently that Cisco actually flinched. "I'm going out there."

"I'm coming with you!" Iris dashed after him.

Cisco shook his head and rubbed his temples. "This is just *not* my best day."

Caitlin patted him on the back. "You're trying your best. This is a trying time."

"Oh, wait until I tell you what I learned in my vibe. You have no idea about *trying time* . . ."

With a quirk of her eyebrows, Caitlin tilted her head. "Oh, really? Do tell."

And Cisco did.

Barry skidded to a halt in the particle accelerator, crackling with electricity, still vibrating, his eyes partially attuned to Earth 27. A crumbling building in that sad version of Central City lingered at the edge of his vision before fading, the particle accelerator solidifying around him. The architecture and the detailing on the machinery were specific to his native universe—he was definitely back home on Earth 1!

He'd been gone much, much longer than he'd intended. The relativistic physics of interdimensional travel meant that the timelines on alternate Earths didn't match up exactly— sometimes it was Tuesday here and Monday on Earth 2, he'd noticed—but his absence had been more protracted than anyone expected. A part of him thought they'd all be waiting for him here, but no.

He dashed up to the Cortex. Caitlin, H.R., and Cisco stood around one of the computer monitors, focused so intently that they didn't react to the gust of wind that preceded his entry.

"Guys? Yoo-hoo!"

H.R. looked up and grinned from ear to ear. "B.A.!" he exclaimed. "You're back! A celebratory quaff is in order!" He downed half a mug of coffee in a single noisy slurp.

"Where's everyone else?" Barry asked.

"Better question is," Cisco said, rounding on Barry and grabbing the torn cowl from his belt, "what did you do to my poor suit? And where have *you* been? You told your mother and me you'd be studying with your friends over on Earth 2, but we checked and you weren't there. Were you off with a bad crowd?"

Barry chuckled, both at Cisco's poor attempt to sound like a parent and at the memories of a very *bad crowd*, indeed. "Long story. Came back here to touch base and have you look at the harness before I try to go back to Earth 2. But first: Catch me up on Earthworm."

Caitlin pushed away from her desk and came to him, arms open. He accepted her hug. It felt good to be back. "Mr. All Business Allen. Let us enjoy you returning from the wilds of the Multiverse."

Cisco grudgingly slapped him on the back. "Yeah, welcome back. Even though you messed up my costume."

"I swear I'll make it up to you with tales of Earth 27."

Cisco considered this and nodded, mollified. Caitlin pulled away. "Iris has been desperate to talk to you. It's about your job. Your hearing is tomorrow, but you haven't even talked to that Frye guy—"

Barry shook his head. "Not now. Where *is* Iris?"

Caitlin looked at Cisco, who looked over at H.R. "I'm not telling him," H.R. said.

"Where is she?" Barry demanded.

"She's fine!" Caitlin said quickly. "Wally is in the sewers, and we sort of, well, lost contact with him."

Barry raised a disturbed eyebrow.

"But Joe and Iris went to check it out," Caitlin said hurriedly. "I'm sure everything is fine."

She didn't sound like she truly believed that, but before Barry could question her further, Cisco jumped in.

"I have some good news, though. I know where Hocus Pocus is from."

That was quite possibly the only bit of information that could distract Barry from asking more questions about Wally and Iris and Joe and Earthworm. "You do?" He held up the wand.

Cisco nodded, his mouth set in a grim line. "Many Bothans died to bring us this information. Dude's from the future."

Suddenly it all made sense, and Barry felt like an idiot

for not realizing sooner. Of course. The super-developed technology, so far beyond anything any of them had ever seen before. Even Pocus's comment when Barry had asked him where he'd come from.

"Where?" Pocus *had said with an obnoxious, knowing chuckle. "I was born not far from here, geographically speaking."*

Geographically speaking. Temporally speaking, though . . .

"The *future*. Like Reverse-Flash."

Cisco waggled an open hand back and forth in a *maybe so, maybe not* gesture. "Not *exactly* like the Reverse-Flash. Ol' Eobard hailed from a mere four or five centuries from now. Our pal Hocus Pocus is from the sixty-fourth century."

Barry blinked. "Say what?"

"That was my reaction, too," H.R. confessed, leaning against a wall. "The numbers just boggle the mind, don't they? I found that three or four cups of Black Ivory coffee help digest the information."

Cisco growled and spun around to H.R. "Do you know how much that stuff *costs*?"

H.R. blinked rapidly. "Can you really put a price on paradise, Francisco?"

As they bantered, Barry shook his head. The sixty-fourth century . . . It was madness. He couldn't even project his imagination that far, couldn't envision what could possibly motivate someone to travel back to the twenty-first century from so far in the future.

Gripping Hocus Pocus's wand, though, he knew that ultimately motivations and centuries didn't matter. Not one bit.

Hocus Pocus had threatened Barry. All of Team Flash. The entire city. In the end, the choice was obvious.

"I'm going to go there," he said.

Caitlin had turned back to her computer—now she froze at the keyboard and slowly rotated her chair to stare at him.

H.R. and Cisco, arguing over the S.T.A.R. Labs budget for coffee, paused and looked over at him.

"Go *where*?" Cisco asked in a tone of voice that said he knew the answer but couldn't believe it.

"Not where—when. The sixty-fourth century."

A moment of silence in the Cortex, with only the soft hiss of the air recirculation system to break the quiet.

"How?" Caitlin asked at last.

Barry smiled. "The same way I do everything else. I'm going to *run* there. I'm going to run four thousand three hundred years into the future!"

NEXT IN

THE FLASH

This is it—it's time to take the battle right to Hocus Pocus on his home turf . . . the sixty-fourth century! The Flash will attempt something he's never tried before and journey into the far, far future. But what truths will he uncover in the days after tomorrow?

Meanwhile, in the present, the rest of Team Flash must work together in order to stop Earthworm before more innocents die. But even if they all succeed at their missions, will Barry Allen still have a job to come back to?

ACKNOWLEDGMENTS

STILL HAVE TO GIVE A SHOUT-OUT TO ALL Flash writers past and present, but this time especially to Gardner Fox, who—with artist Mike Sekowsky—first unleashed the Crime Syndicate of America on unsuspecting readers and gave us a Johnny Quick we could really hate.

Once again, I am so grateful to the folks at Warner Bros. and The CW who made this book possible, especially Amy Weingartner and Josh Anderson, Greg Berlanti, Todd Helbing, Sarah Schechter, Carl Ogawa, Lindsay Kiesel, Janice Aguilar-Herrero, Catherine Shin, Thomas Zellers, Kristin Chin.

And my undying thanks to the hardworking crew at Abrams—including but not limited to Andrew Smith, Richard Slovak, Maggie Lehrman, Pamela Bobowicz, Chad Beckerman, Evangelos Vasilakis, Alison Gervais, Melanie Chang, Maya Bradford, and Liz Fithian. And pour one out for Orlando Dos Reis, editor-in-absentia.

And César Moreno! How about that cover? Holy cow! Wow! César!

Last but never least: My wife and my kids and their eternal patience as Daddy disappears into the office and into another universe far, far too often. I love you all.

ABOUT THE AUTHOR

BARRY LYGA is the author of the *New York Times* bestselling I Hunt Killers series and many other critically acclaimed middle-grade and young adult novels. A self-proclaimed Flash fanatic, Barry lives and podcasts near New York City with his family. Find him online at barrylyga.com.

READ ON FOR A

SUPE

SNEAK PEEK OF

RGIRL™

SE OF THE ANCIENTS

BY JO WHITTEMORE

My name is Kara Zor-El. When I was a child, my planet, Krypton, was dying. I was sent to Earth to protect my cousin, but my pod got knocked off course, and by the time I got here, my cousin had already grown up and become Superman. I hid who I really was until one day when an accident forced me to reveal myself to the world.

To most people, I'm Kara Danvers, a reporter at CatCo Worldwide Media. But in secret, I work with my adoptive sister, Alex, for the Department of Extra-Normal Operations to protect my city from alien life and anyone else that means to cause it harm. I am . . . Supergirl!

PREVIOUSLY IN SUPERGIRL

National City has seen its share of trouble. But weeks ago, a rare Atlantean metal, orichalcum, was released into the air after an explosion. Regular citizens began to exhibit superpowers with enough force to rival National City's own hero—Supergirl. She and her friends at CatCo and the DEO had their work cut out for them. The orichalcum gave these supercitizens enough power to wage an epic battle. But thanks to Supergirl's quick thinking, and a little superpower that too often goes unnoticed—logic—the supercitizens were defeated. The orichalcum was returned to Atlantis, along with its guardian. And National City returned to its normal, quiet pace, with only one superhero at the ready when she's needed.

But there is always quiet before the chaos . . .

Things have been quiet in national city ever since.

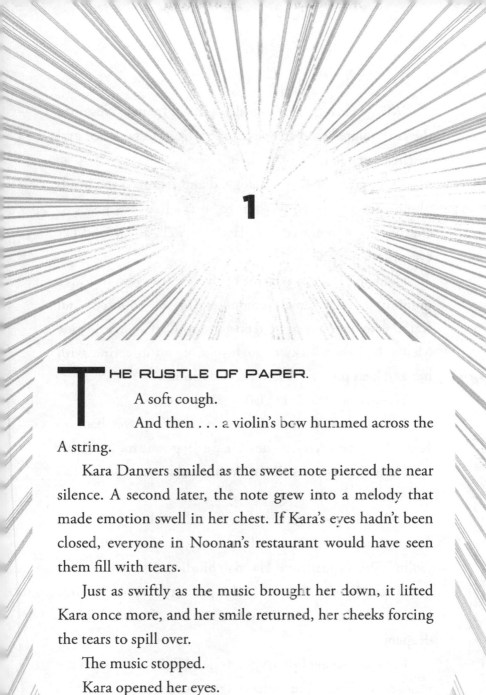

1

THE RUSTLE OF PAPER.

A soft cough.

And then . . . a violin's bow hummed across the A string.

Kara Danvers smiled as the sweet note pierced the near silence. A second later, the note grew into a melody that made emotion swell in her chest. If Kara's eyes hadn't been closed, everyone in Noonan's restaurant would have seen them fill with tears.

Just as swiftly as the music brought her down, it lifted Kara once more, and her smile returned, her cheeks forcing the tears to spill over.

The music stopped.

Kara opened her eyes.

"Miss Danvers, are you all right?" Hannah Nesmith, the curly-haired woman seated across from Kara, asked and reached out a hand.

"Oh, gosh, yes!" Kara laughed and removed the head-phones she was wearing. "I'm so sorry. That was just . . . amazing." She removed her glasses, as well, and wiped her eyes with a napkin.

Hannah Nesmith was one of the few (too few, in Kara's opinion) famous female composers in the country. And Kara, who worked as a reporter for CatCo Worldwide Media, had been lucky enough to score an interview with her and hear one of her latest compositions.

Hannah smiled. "I'm glad you enjoyed it."

Kara passed the headphones and music player back to Hannah. "Seriously. I have never had a song *move* me like that!"

Hannah pointed at Kara. "You should hear it with a full orchestra."

"Oh, I don't think there'd be enough napkins," Kara said with a chuckle. "And bravo, by the way, for your skill on the violin." She clapped, and Hannah blushed.

"I actually play the flute in this piece; the person you just heard was Claude." As she said the name, Hannah's blush deepened.

Kara pursed her lips. "A good friend?" she asked with the innocence of someone pretending not to pry.

Hannah smirked at her. "You could say that. We play for the same orchestra, but we met during a triathlon."

Kara's jaw dropped. "Hold up! You're a ridiculously talented composer, musician, *and* triathlete?" She leaned toward Hannah and whispered, "Are *you* Supergirl?"

Hannah shrugged and laughed. "Maybe. She and I are never in the same place at the same time."

Kara laughed, too. *If only you knew you were sitting right across the table from her,* she thought.

Kara probed Hannah about her triathlon hobby, which had, in turn, led to Hannah's inventing an app for note-taking on the go. Kara flipped through the notes *she'd* just taken on a steno pad, shaking her head.

"Hannah, I would seriously kill for a fraction of your talent," she said.

"Oh, please. You and I aren't so different," Hannah said. "We're both writers who speak to people through our work."

Kara snorted. "Yeah, but *my* work doesn't sell out shows at National City Music Hall."

"But it could sell out a TED Talk," Hannah replied. "By this time next year, you could be in Vancouver, giving a speech on women in media."

Kara smiled. "I don't see myself going to Vancouver."

Their server arrived with the bill, and Kara plucked the check holder away before Hannah could reach it.

"Dinner is on CatCo," she said, even though she was pretty sure her boss, Snapper, would scoff at the idea. She'd once seen him drink from a coffee cup labeled "~~No More~~ Never Mr. Nice Guy."

Kara extended a hand to Hannah, who shook it. "This was such an honor, Ms. Nesmith. Thank you for meeting me so late in the day."

"Anytime," said Hannah. She leaned toward Kara. "And even though the performances are sold out, I've got VIP passes, so if you want to come with someone special . . ."

Kara smiled. Her someone special was Mon-El of Daxam, but his home world had been a party planet, where people were unlikely to listen to classical music. Anything without inappropriate lyrics was probably not going to be on his radar. Still, Mon-El had been spending a lot of time at National City Museum learning about ancient civilizations. Maybe Kara could convince him to expand his interests to classical music as well.

"I'd love to go," Kara told Hannah. "Thank you."

"I'll leave two tickets at Will Call," Hannah said. She glanced at her watch and grimaced. "I hate to eat and run, but I've got another appointment."

"Yes, go, go!" Kara waved her away and placed some money in the check holder.

Hannah smiled gratefully and rose from her chair, col-

244

liding with a tall, sleek-haired brunette. Kara perked up when she realized it was one of her best friends, Lena Luthor.

"Oh! I'm terribly sorry. Are you all right?" Lena reached for Hannah's arm, and her eyes widened. "Hannah Nesmith! What are you doing here, of all places?"

"I just finished an interview with *CatCo* magazine," said Hannah, gesturing to Kara. "This is—"

Lena's face brightened. "Kara!" She opened her arms, and Kara stood and stepped into them, smiling.

"Hey, you! What are *you* doing here?"

They separated, and Lena nodded to a nearby table of suit-clad men and women. "I'm at a business dinner as well." In a lower voice, she added, "I'm hoping they'll fund a cancer cure I'm developing."

Hannah Nesmith laughed and shook her head. "Leave it to you to find a cure for cancer, Lena." She turned to Kara. "You want to talk talent? Back in school, Lena was a fencing master, a Chess Federation champ, *and* she finished two MIT Mystery Hunts in under twenty-four hours." She elbowed Lena. "But you left the coins for other people to find. So sweet."

Lena ducked her head. "You speak too kindly of me, Hannah." She squeezed her hands. "Are you in town for a bit?"

Hannah nodded. "I'm at the Wayward Arms if you want to catch up."

"I'd love that!" Lena's eyes flitted back to her table. "And now, I really must dash."

"Go get 'em!" Kara cheered.

Lena winked and hurried off.

"I'm afraid I have to go, too," Hannah told Kara. "If you have any more questions, please feel free to call." With a wave, she departed.

Kara watched both women walk away, visionaries and dynamos of the twenty-first century. Back when Kara had been Cat Grant's coffee-fetching assistant, Lena and Hannah had already been wowing the world with their talents.

The thought made Kara feel a bit . . . unimpressive.

Yes, she was Supergirl, but that was a secret she couldn't share. As Kara Danvers, she'd finally moved on from being an office assistant, but she was a barely recognized reporter.

Meanwhile, Hannah Nesmith was running triathlons, inventing apps, and composing symphonies, while Lena Luthor was mastering anything she even glanced at.

Neither Supergirl nor Kara Danvers could compare.